HOME SWEET DRAMA

Other books in the
CANTERWOOD CREST SERIES:

TAKE THE REINS

CHASING BLUE

BEHIND THE BIT

TRIPLE FAULT

BEST ENEMIES

LITTLE WHITE LIES

RIVAL REVENGE

Canterwood Crest

HOME SWEET DRAMA

JESSICA BURKHART

ALADDIN M!X

New York London Toronto Sydney

ALADDIN M!X

Simon & Schuster Children's Publishing Division

1230 Avenue of the Americas, New York, NY 10020

First Aladdin M!X edition April 2010

Copyright © 2010 by Jessica Burkhart

All rights reserved, including the right of reproduction
in whole or in part in any form.

ALADDIN is a trademark of Simon & Schuster, Inc., and related logo
is a registered trademark of Simon & Schuster, Inc.

ALADDIN M!X and related logo are registered trademarks
of Simon & Schuster, Inc.

For information about special discounts for bulk purchases, please
contact Simon & Schuster Special Sales at 1-866-506-1949
or business@simonandschuster.com.

The Simon & Schuster Speakers Bureau can bring authors to your live event.
For more information or to book an event contact the Simon & Schuster Speakers
Bureau at 1-866-248-3049 or visit our website at www.simonspeakers.com.

Designed by Jessica Handelman

The text of this book was set in Venetian 301 BT.

Manufactured in the United States of America

6 8 10 9 7

Library of Congress Control Number 2009942965

ISBN 978-1-4169-9040-6

ISBN 978-1-4169-9909-6 (eBook)

1113 OFF

To girls' nights—always legen- . . . *wait for it* . . . *-dary!*

ACKNOWLEDGMENTS

Thanks to *How I Met Your Mother*'s Barney for uttering that epic line.

Thank you, Alyssa Henkin, for representing this project.

Lots of thanks to Monica Stevenson and the amazing Canterwood models.

On the S&S Team of Awesome: Jessica Handelman, Liesa Abrams, Russell Gordon, Karin Paprocki, Alyson Heller, Mara Anastas, Fiona Simpson, Bethany Buck, Bess Braswell, Lucille Rettino, Nicole Russo, and Venessa Williams. Brenna Franzitta, thank you so much for being a fab managing ed.

Kate Angelella, the edit letter for this book is by far the most memorable. I hope you realize what you (fueled by coffee, espresso beans, and Red Bull) bring to these books. You're not only a fabulous editor, but also an envy-worthy writer, and that's what gives your edits that extra sparkle.

Thanks to my awesome reader girlies! Your e-mails, letters, and comments mean so much. Team Canterwood!

Mandy Morgan and Lauren Barnholdt, the phone calls and e-mails are so fun, and I always look forward to chatting.

Ross Angelella, thanks for introducing me to the ICB. A perfect "I finished my draft!" reward. Or, you know, a Monday night "just because." ;)

KAA, I *always* get stuck writing yours. Sparkly spritzers, nights at BF, falling down (we really need to start that photo-journal . . .) and *HIMYM* marathons are just *some* of the things that make you beyond superimportant in my life. And there's so much more to do . . . LYSMB <3

HOME SWEET DRAMA

I

TO JASMINE

JULIA AND ALISON'S REVENGE WAS COMPLETE.
They'd taken out the biggest threat at school.

Jasmine King had been expelled from Canterwood
Crest Academy.

I'd been standing in Jasmine's empty dorm room for a
long time. Just staring.

I leaned my back against the wall and drew my knees
to my chest, lowering myself to the bare wooden floor—
shaking my head in amazement. It had happened so fast.
I'd gone to the indoor arena to practice and had been
using Mr. Conner's camera to film my session. Jas hadn't
known the camera was on and she'd started to brag about
how she'd framed Julia and Alison by making it look as if
they'd cheated on their history test. I'd texted Julia and

Alison about the tape and they'd taken it to the headmistress. I'd just left the Trio's suite after a this-close-to-tears Heather had thanked me for saving her friends.

Jas was gone. I remembered her moving into my dorm and how I'd felt—I'd hated that she had transferred from Wellington Prep to Canterwood. It felt like she'd done it just to torture the Trio and me with her presence. Now, there was no trace of her in her old room. It was as if she'd never existed. Part of me felt a little sorry for her that she'd been yanked away to a new school, but mostly, I didn't care. She deserved what she got for everything she'd done to us.

I reached for my phone to text Julia, Alison, and Heather. Everything had happened in an instant—Heather probably had no clue that Jasmine had been expelled. But before I could start a text, my phone buzzed.

Come 2 r suite & celebrate. ~H

That almost made me laugh out loud. Of course Heather knew. I should have known that. She was aware of everything that went on at school.

K. B there in a sec. I sent my text.

I got up and stuck my head of out the doorway and looked down the hallway toward my room. I'd planned to spend the rest of the evening with Paige, my BFF and roommate, but I couldn't say no to celebrating Jas's departure—something I'd hoped for since the day she'd arrived. I stepped out of Jas's old room and left the door wide open behind me.

I left Winchester and walked back toward Orchard. I hurried, then caught myself. I surely wasn't excited about hanging out with the Trio—it was just glee over Jasmine. Right? But maybe a tiny part of me wanted to hang with them. We still weren't friends, but things had sort of changed.

I walked across campus and marveled at how gorgeous it was, especially with the fiery orange-red sunset. The manicured lawns were trimmed like golf course grass and the dark lacquered fence rails gleamed. Every inch of the winding sidewalks looked as if someone had just swept them. No matter how many times I crossed the campus, it never felt any less prestigious. There was a reputation to uphold as one of the top East Coast boarding schools.

When I got to Orchard Hall, I stared at it for a minute. The brick building was four stories tall and each window had a stark white frame with a small ledge underneath. Black shutters on either side contrasted with the frames and the rooms on the top floor had peaks over the windows. Two chimneys rose from the back of the building. A black old-fashioned street lantern was on each side of the

front of the building. Soon, their light would illuminate the heavy wooden door that led into the dorm hall.

I took a breath before opening the door. Callie, my ex-BFF lived here, and the last thing I wanted was to run into her. But I pushed the thoughts away—tonight wasn't about Callie—it was about celebrating Jasmine's exit from Canterwood.

I walked down the glossy wooden floor and stopped in front of the Trio's door. I'd barely knocked when a bouncy Alison pulled the door open.

"Sasha!" she said, grabbing me in a hug.

"I'm so happy for you," I said. She let me go and I walked into Julia, Heather, and Alison's living room. "You can start riding tomorrow."

From her spot on the couch, Julia smiled at me. "Yeah, I bet we can." She took a breath, glancing down before looking back up at me. "Thanks."

I nodded. "I'm sorry I didn't believe you before."

Julia shook her head. "Don't be dumb. You're the one who saved us—you don't have to apologize for anything."

Heather appeared from her room and motioned for me to sit on the couch. On the coffee table in front of us, there was a bottle of ginger ale and four plastic champagne flutes.

"Let's toast," Heather said. She tossed her long blond hair over one shoulder and sat beside me. Julia poured ginger ale into all of our flutes and we raised them.

"To Jasmine," Heather said.

"To Jasmine," I echoed with the Trio.

2
DEARLY DEPARTED

AS WE SIPPED OUR GINGER ALE, I REALIZED I hadn't been this relaxed in a while. Julia and Alison both had permanent grins on their faces and Heather hadn't lost her satisfied smile since I'd arrived. She sat cross-legged on the couch and pulled out her cell.

"This definitely calls for pizza," she said. She ordered a large half-cheese, half-pepperoni and snapped her phone shut.

Alison brushed a long lock of sandy brown hair off her face. "I almost can't believe it. She's gone. Jasmine isn't coming back."

"How did you find out so fast?" I asked. "I was in her room when Heather texted me. I was totally shocked that you knew."

"Please, Silver," Heather said, rolling her eyes. "We know about stuff at Canterwood *before* it happens."

"That's kind of true." I almost shuddered. "Ugh, I was in her room thinking about the day she moved in. I thought I'd spend the rest of the year walking by her door or running into her in the common room. It would have been awful."

Alison nodded. "You probably wanted to switch dorms when she moved into Winchester."

"Almost," I said. "It's going to take me a while not to look for her."

"Get used to it," Julia said. "She's *never* coming back."

"Ever," Heather said. "I mean, where's she going to go? I'd be surprised if Wellington took her back. But her parents have tons of money, so they'll probably buy her way back into the school if they have to."

Alison rolled her eyes. "Whatever. I don't care where she goes as long as she's not here."

We smiled at each other. It was surprising at how comfortable I felt in their suite. They'd somehow managed to get a triple with three separate bedrooms, a small living room, and a tiny kitchen area. As far as I knew, no other eighth graders had those.

Someone knocked on the door and Julia jumped up

off the couch to answer it. It was Stephanie, the Orchard dorm monitor, with the pizza. She smiled and handed the steaming box to Julia.

"Hi, Sasha," she said. "Nice to see you again."

I'd slept over the other night, ironically, to escape Jasmine and her stalking me in Winchester.

"You too," I said.

Stephanie smiled at us and left. Alison grabbed plates and napkins and we dug into the pizza.

Heather put down her slice of pepperoni and glanced at us—her blue eyes shining. "Let's play a game," she said. "In honor of our dearly departed, let's talk about all the horrible things Jas did when she was here."

"Ooh, definitely," Alison said. "I've already got one."

Heather motioned for her to go.

"Befriending the Belles," Alison said. "*That* was dumb on so many levels."

"Uh, for sure," Julia said. She shook her head. "She really thought they wanted to be her friends. No matter how much help she assumed they'd be in going after us, she had to know they'd get bored and ditch her eventually."

We all nodded.

"I know one," Julia said. "When she decided to try to

intimidate all of us at the show before she'd even come to Canterwood."

"That was so lame," I said. "She made us all mad at her. Plus, it didn't help her at all that Heather already knew what kind of competitor she was. Talking trash and trying to freak us out was dumb."

Heather took a bite of her pizza. "That's for sure. And she didn't stop there at that show, either. Remember when she poured oil on Aristocrat and I almost missed my class?"

"Yeah!" Alison said, rolling her eyes. "And Sasha helped you."

"And when she 'accidentally' spilled molasses on my hair during Mr. Bright's class?" I added. "Classy."

"So her style," Julia said. "She's obvi got a thing for dumping things on people and animals."

"I've got another one," I said. "A good one." Everyone looked at me, waiting for my answer. "The day she decided to come to Canterwood was her biggest mistake ever."

And to that, we all raised our flutes and clinked them together. We fell into happy silence—everyone was probably going through Jasmine memories in their heads. It still didn't feel real.

"I wish I'd been there when Headmistress Drake told her she was expelled," Julia said.

"Yeaaah," Alison said, sighing. "*That* would have been amazing."

"Jasmine walked into Headmistress Drake's office probably expecting to be told she'd won an award or was just all-around awesome," Heather said, rolling her eyes.

"I bet she almost passed out when the headmistress showed her the tape," Julia said. "I hope she felt the way Alison and I did when we were hauled out of class for cheating."

"There's no way she expected it," I said. "She thought she got away with it and she was waiting for a chance to go after Heather or me next."

"You're lucky she got expelled instead of suspended or something less serious," Heather said. "Otherwise, she wouldn't have been after *me*. She would have gone after you for getting her in trouble."

Heather was right. Jas definitely would have tried everything she could to get me out of Canterwood.

"Forget about that," Heather said. "Jasmine King is gone. Let's go back to the fun part—imagining how she reacted to getting kicked out."

And we spent the next hour doing just that. After our

zillionth recount of what we thought had happened, I remembered I hadn't been back to my room for a long time.

"I better go," I said. "Paige is probably wondering where I am."

But as I stood, I was reluctant to leave. I liked their cozy living room, and maybe . . . I even liked hanging out with them.

"Don't stay up all night," Heather said, giving me her signature *you-better-listen-or-else* look. "We've got our taping for Mr. Nicholson tomorrow."

I'd forgotten about that for a couple of hours after stressing about it nonstop for days. Mr. Nicholson was the head scout for the Youth Equestrian National Team—the YENT—and our coach, Mr. Conner, had to update him with a progress report via video on our riding.

"I won't," I said. "See you."

"And Homecoming starts tomorrow," Alison said, her brown eyes wide. "Try not to think about it or you won't be able to sleep."

I caught Heather's eye and we shared a look. Neither of us were into Homecoming—any of it—and we both wanted this week to go by fast so we could get to fall break on Saturday. I was going to spend a wonderful week in Manhattan with Paige. Getting away from campus couldn't come too soon.

I left their room smiling but then a disturbing thought occurred to me—were the Trio and I becoming . . . friends?

3

AVOID HOMECOMING
OR DIE

WHEN I WALKED PAST JAS'S DOOR FOR THE second time, it was shut tight. I smiled as I walked by and opened the door to my room. Paige dashed in front of me, hopping up and down.

"Omigod," she said. "I have the most *amazing* news ever!"

"Me too!" I said.

We grinned at each other. "You go first," I said.

"No, you," Paige said.

I shook my head. "You were the first to say you had news. Go."

Paige grabbed my hand and pulled me onto her bed. "Okay! Okay! I'll go."

I looked at her flushed face and had a feeling what this was about.

"I. Kissed. Ryan," Paige said. She covered her face with her hands, blushing, then glanced up at me. "We kissed!"

"Ohhhhmiiiigod!" I screamed. "Paige! You and Ryan! You kissed Ryan. That's so amazing. Tell me everything."

Paige's smile was huge. "He asked me to the Sweet Shoppe and when we were leaving, he held my hand. It was so sweet. Then, he walked me back to Winchester. We stopped at the bottom of the stairs and he looked at me and I just *knew*. I remembered you telling me about your first kiss with Jacob and how you had that feeling?"

I nodded. "Yep. You just know."

Paige got up and started walking around our room. "So he took both of my hands and looked at me. We leaned in at the same time and . . . kissed."

"Was it perfect?" I asked.

"Beyond perfect," Paige said. "Sooo amazing. I thought I'd be nervous and worried about doing it wrong, but it was so special."

I smiled at her. "That's awesome, Paige. I'm so, so happy for you."

Paige sat back on the end of her bed. "And that's not even the best part. When I was about to go inside, he asked me to be his girlfriend!"

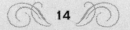

"I knew he would!" I said. "You've got a boyfriend, Paige Parker. A boyfriend!"

Paige shook her head like she didn't believe it. "I know. But it's so weird. I can't even process it." She played with the ends of her red-gold hair. "I have a boyfriend."

I hadn't felt this excited for her in a long time. Paige deserved this.

"Now spill your news!" Paige said. "I need to know!"

I smiled. "Well, it's not as exciting as getting your first boyfriend, but it's pretty close."

Paige leaned forward. "C'mon already!'

I wanted to build it up, but I couldn't help myself.

"Jasmine got expelled," I said. "She's gone."

Paige's mouth fell open in what looked like a scene from a teen movie we'd mock. "What?"

"It's insane. I was riding in the arena with Mr. Conner's camera on. I caught her on tape confessing to framing Julia and Alison for cheating. They got the tape and when I came back to go to our room a couple of hours ago, all of her stuff was gone."

"Wow," Paige whispered. "I feel awful for Julia and Alison because they've missed all of that time riding, but . . . Jas getting thrown out, just like that. Can you imagine?"

I shrugged. "Who cares? She framed them and she got

caught. She's *gone*. We never have to see her again. Ever."

Paige nodded. "Yeah. True. I just wonder where she's going to go. And you found out a couple of hours ago. Where'd you disappear to?"

I paused for a second. "The Trio's. We were celebrating."

"Oh," Paige said. "That makes sense." She looked down at her lap and twisted the silver ring on her index finger.

Paige was definitely not as thrilled as I thought she'd be.

"We're *all* so happy," I said. "She was our biggest competition and she made every lesson awful."

"I know, I know," Paige said. "You're right. I'm really glad she's not going to be stressing you all out anymore."

"Exactly."

Paige was quiet for a few seconds, her head bent down. "So, the truth about Julia and Alison finally came out." She paused. "You think anything else might?"

"Like what?" I pretended I had no idea what she was talking about. She needed to stop going there.

Paige locked eyes with me. "I don't know, like maybe the truth about what happened at your party?"

I got up and pulled open my closet door, searching for pajamas. "Paige, let's not do this again. You promised you were done talking about it. We both had awesome things happen today, so let's just enjoy it, okay?"

I turned away from my closet and faced Paige.

"You're right." Paige shrugged. "Sorry I brought it up."

But I could tell by the tone in her voice that she wasn't too sorry. She still didn't believe that I'd tried to kiss Jacob, Callie's boyfriend, at my birthday party. And she was right—he'd tried to kiss me. But Eric, my then-boyfriend, had caught me with my hands on Jacob's chest. I'd been pushing Jacob away, but Eric had thought it was something else. Pain burned in my throat. I still cared about Eric and I'd hurt him so much. I knew there was no way we'd ever get back together.

I tossed my pj's on my bed and opened my laptop. Beside my computer was the egg Jacob and I were "parenting" for health class. I couldn't help but smile when I looked at the goofy face he'd drawn on it. I stared at the face for a second. I hated hiding this secret from Paige—it was hurting our friendship. Since my birthday party I'd been set on never telling her the truth, but how long could I keep it from my best friend? If I told her the truth about my party, she'd be there for me—listening and offering advice. Maybe I'd been making that mistake all along. Maybe I needed to tell her.

I looked back at my computer. I wanted to check my

e-mail to see if there were any schedule changes for the week since it was Homecoming. I logged in and clicked on *Homecoming schedule* in my inbox. I opened the e-mail.

"Did you see this?" I asked Paige, pointing to my screen. I needed a light topic of conversation to ease the tension.

She walked over and stood behind me. Silently, we both read the e-mail from Headmistress Drake.

Dear Students of Canterwood Crest Academy:

It is with great pleasure that I present a list of activities for this year's Homecoming. Though the schedule changes from year to year, the tradition of Canterwood Crest's Homecoming remains the same. This week is a chance for you to show your support and loyalty to our fine institution. Please review the list below and I hope your schedule allows you to participate as often as possible. I look forward to honoring Canterwood Crest with my students.

Sincerely,

Headmistress Drake

Homecoming Week Activities:

Monday: Physical competition after lunch periods

Tuesday: Crazy dress day

Wednesday: Bonfire

Thursday: Green-and-gold day, pep rally and football game

Friday: Dance

The rest of the e-mail listed the nominees for each grade and I tried not to roll my eyes when I read *8th-grade nominees—Sasha Silver, Paige Parker, Heather Fox, Nicole Allen, Callie Harper, Jacob Schwartz, Eric Rodriguez, Troy Brown, Ben Wells, and Ryan Shore.*

"Omigod—look at all of that stuff!" Paige said. "A pep rally, the dance, contests—it's going to be *awesome.*"

"Yeah," I said, trying to keep my voice cheery.

I closed my laptop—not wanting to look at the e-mail for another second. Even the font was hunter green and gold—our school colors. I couldn't have been less interested in Homecoming. The last thing I wanted was to see Jacob and Callie together. Plus, Eric would definitely go and if he brought a date . . . also something I didn't want to see.

The absolute worst part about my avoid-Homecoming-or-die plan?

I'd been nominated for Homecoming princess.

4

AND THE MADNESS BEGINS

MONDAY MORNINGS WERE ALWAYS KIND OF awful just because they were Mondays, but Paige and I had been waiting for English class to start and I already knew today was going to be bad. The chatter about Homecoming would not stop. There had even been an endless announcement over the loudspeaker during breakfast about how Monday was the first day of Homecoming week and blah, blah, blah.

"Omigod, did you get a dress yet? You did, right?"

"Tyler already asked me to the dance!"

"I look *awful* in everything. I've got to find the *perfect* dress or I'll die."

I tried to read my notes on *The Secret Garden* for Mr. Davidson's English class, but I couldn't tune out the talk.

It made things worse because the classroom wasn't set up in the typical way. There were only ten of us since it was an advanced class. Instead of desks, Mr. Davidson had arranged comfy chairs in a circle and I couldn't help but hear E-V-E-R-Y word about Homecoming.

I looked up when Alison walked in and took a seat beside Paige. Alison and I smiled at each other, then Alison saw the sparkly purple notebook on Paige's lap. At the top of the page HOMECOMING was written in bubble font and Paige was making notes. She'd written *Things 2 get 4 decorations* as the first thing on her list.

"You're helping decorate?" Alison asked Paige. Her voice was way louder than necessary.

"Of course!" Paige said. "It's *Homecoming*."

"I'm decorating too," Alison said. "Omigod, everything's going to look fabulous. Totally green and gold, but not too much so that it's, like, tacky."

Paige nodded. "Exactly. I've got a list of ideas. Want to see?"

Alison clapped her hands together. "Show me."

I just couldn't believe it. Even Paige and Alison were bonding over Homecoming.

"Hey, P," I said.

She looked away from Alison. "Yeah?"

"Can we talk later? There's something I want to—"

"Paige!" Alison interrupted.

Paige looked away from me and Alison pointed to a note on Paige's paper.

"You're going to use gold glitter on the tables?" Alison asked. "Omigod. Love."

Paige looked back at me and started to say something, but Mr. Davidson walked into the classroom. He picked up a file from his desk and a worn copy of *The Secret Garden*, then took his seat.

"We'll talk later," Paige whispered.

Sure we would. *After* she did whatever she was doing for Homecoming.

"Happy Monday, class," he said in a teasing voice. "I hope you all had a good weekend and I especially hope you enjoyed reading the assigned chapters. Let's get the discussion started. Vanessa, please tell us what you thought about the reading."

Vanessa blushed and, looking down, started fumbling through her papers. "Um, I, well, I . . ." She let her sentence trail off. "I thought it was good."

"Good how?" Mr. Davidson asked. His kept his eyes on Vanessa.

Vanessa's pink face brightened to red. "It was good

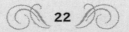

because . . . the chapters weren't boring. And the story was interesting. So it wasn't . . . uh, boring."

Mr. Davidson narrowed his gaze. "Vanessa, did you complete the reading?"

"No," Vanessa whispered. "I'm sorry."

"You know my rule about this class," Mr. Davidson said. "Anyone who has not done the reading and cannot participate gets a zero for the day. Normally, I'd ask you to leave, but since is the first time you haven't done your homework, I'll allow you to stay."

Vanessa blushed and looked down at her lap.

Mr. Davidson looked at Mandy. "Mandy?"

She shook her head. "I didn't read either, Mr. Davidson. I'm sorry. I got so busy with prepping for Homecoming."

Mr. Davidson frowned and shifted his gaze among all of us. "How many of you completed the reading? Let me reiterate—the *assigned* reading."

Only one guy and I raised our hands. I looked over at Paige and her head was down. Paige had *never* skipped doing her homework. Was Homecoming making everyone crazy?

"This is unacceptable," Mr. Davidson said. "I realize it's Homecoming, but that is not an excuse for any of you to skip classwork. Those of you who did not do the reading will stay and read through the rest of the class period."

He looked at me. "Sasha, after you and Aaron share your thoughts on the reading with the class, you're both free to go."

Major. Score.

I looked down at my notes. "Well . . . ," I started.

After I finished, Aaron offered his opinion and Mr. Davidson asked us both a few questions. Then he motioned to the door.

"You're both free to go," he said.

I gathered my books and papers and shot Paige a sympathetic look. Everyone's eyes were on Aaron and me as we left the classroom. I left the building and plopped my bookbag on a bench shaded by an oak tree.

"Ugh," I said aloud.

It was going to be hard to force myself to go back to class after the half hour break was over. I wished I could sit outside all day, but I had many more classes to go. *Ignore it for now,* I told myself. *And just enjoy the break.*

I pulled out my phone, thinking now was the perfect time to call Mom. We hadn't talked in a while and since she was working at the library, she'd only have a few minutes to chat, so we wouldn't have to talk for too long.

I knew she'd want to ask me a zillion questions about Homecoming, but I was determined to keep the convo on other things.

I dialed her number and waited.

"This is Gail Silver speaking," she said.

"Hi, Mom," I said.

"Sasha! Hi, hon," Mom said. "Why aren't you in class?"

"Our class let out early," I said. I wasn't going to tell her I'd been excused because I'd been the only girl focused on school instead of the H-word.

"I'm glad you get a break. That's nice. How's your day?" Mom asked.

I could hear the beeping of books being checked out.

"Great," I said. "Paige and I are going to start planning for fall break later."

That would definitely distract Mom from asking about Homecoming.

"I'm so excited that you're staying with Paige in New York City," Mom said. "You're going to have such a wonderful time. You loved it so much when you visited her this summer."

I laughed. "I'm only going to be there a week, Mom. But I'll be sure to get you and Dad souvenirs."

It was Mom's turn to laugh. "Sounds good, hon. And Dad and I will find you something special while we're away. The bed-and-breakfast place we're staying at in Maine looks absolutely charming, just like the town. We'll be sure to find something you like."

"Thanks, Mom," I said. "I've got to study, but I'll e-mail you tomorrow."

"Bye, sweetie," Mom said.

We hung up and I spent the rest of the period dreading going back to class.

I dragged myself back to class and, by some miracle, managed to tune out Homecoming talk for the rest of the day. Just like in Mr. Davidson's class, so few people had prepared for the reading that it made me look good. I crossed my fingers that my teachers would remember it if I ever needed an extension.

In the lunch line I ordered veggie soup and grabbed a handful of cracker packets. I started toward the Trio's table. I paused midstep, wondering if I should sit with Paige. She *was* my best friend and I *had* been sitting with Heather, Julia, and Alison a lot lately. But it was only because there was seriously less tension sitting with them than with Paige. Paige wasn't trying to upset me, but she did, every time she brought up my birthday party. Or Homecoming. Julia and Alison talked about Homecoming, too, but at least I had solidarity with Heather.

I put my tray down across from Heather's and noticed Julia and Alison staring at a sheet of paper on the table. They seemed überabsorbed in it.

"What're you reading?" I asked.

Heather sighed. "You shouldn't have asked. It's the lovely schedule that we all got about Homecoming."

"The lunch activity is ridic," Julia said. "The guys and girls are supposed to have physical contests. The one for us? Jumping rope until we have to stop." She fake-gagged. "I don't think so."

"We're supposed to jump rope until we can't do it anymore or until the period ends," Alison said. "Lame, right?"

Heather snorted. "You think? That's the worst contest I've ever heard. Not that I care, but what're the boys doing?"

I crushed a handful of crackers into my soup and watched Alison scan the paper.

"They're having a push-up contest in the gym in twenty minutes," Alison said. "I'm *not* jumping rope, so I guess we could go watch them."

Heather put her face in her hands for a second, then looked up at Alison, Julia, and me. "Puh-lease. We're not going to watch. We're going to *participate*."

"Yeah!" Julia said. "Why let the boys do a real contest? We can do push-ups too."

"I'm in," I said.

"Let's finish eating and go," Heather said.

We hurried through the rest of our meal—Heather downed her grilled cheese, Alison finished her turkey sub, and Julia's BLT disappeared in minutes. We gathered our trays and I realized I hadn't looked up once from our table. I glanced around as I got up and didn't see Jacob or Callie. Paige was sitting at the center table and looked at me as I walked by.

"If you're heading to the jump-rope contest," she said, "I'm ready and I'll walk with you."

I stopped and so did Julia, Alison, and Heather.

"Actually, we're going to do push-ups," I said.

"Jumping rope is so whatever," Heather said. "If the boys are doing push-ups, so are we."

Paige looked at Geena, then back at us. "Oh, okay. Well, Geena and I are jumping rope. I guess we'll see you at the gym."

This was so weird! Paige and I usually did everything together. Now, I was going with the Trio.

"Yeah. See you there."

I walked away from Paige and followed the Trio out of the caf. We crossed the lawn and I tried not to look at the Homecoming banners and yard signs that kept popping up everywhere.

"At least Homecoming Court nominees aren't allowed to make signs and flyers on top of the ones already advertising the activities," Heather said. "Otherwise, I'd vomit."

"Me too," I said, laughing. "They'd be everywhere trying to get votes."

Julia and Alison were almost jogging now, so far ahead of us in their rush to get to the gym.

"It just means people get more creative," Heather said. "They do all the verbal bribing and campaigning they can."

"Don't forget the threats and blackmail," I said jokingly.

"Def," Heather said. I looked over at her and knew she wasn't kidding. Nominations were prob serious around here. If Heather had really wanted to win, she'd use everything she had to make sure it happened. She'd intimidate people for votes. Lucky for our grade that being Homecoming princess was the last thing she wanted.

"So, you hate Homecoming as much as I do," I said. "But you never said why. You know I do because of the . . . situation, but why don't you like it?"

Heather took a deep breath through her nose and

glanced at me. "My mom was Homecoming queen in high school," she said. "She loves everything about it and she still has her tiara from when she won. She was, like, obsessed with it."

I just nodded.

"She wants me to be princess *so* bad," Heather said. "I've never been into any of it and she knows it, but she never listens. At least my dad gets that I'm an athlete. But my mom . . ." Heather shrugged.

"Doesn't get that her daughter would rather wear paddock boots than heels, right?" I asked.

"Something like that."

I felt bad for Heather. Her dad pressured her to ride all the time and her mom was trying to turn her into a school princess. Now it made sense why Heather hated every aspect of Homecoming.

We reached the gym and walked across the shiny hardwood floor, our shoes squeaking.

I didn't take gym because of the equestrian team, but someone who looked like a gym teacher walked up to us. The velour track suit and whistle around her neck kind of gave her away.

"Girls, go grab jump ropes," she said. "Your competition starts in five minutes."

"We're not here to jump rope," Heather said, stepping forward. She oozed the confidence I wished I had. Her shoulders were back and her voice was firm. "We're doing push-ups."

The woman's head tilted and she stared at us like she thought we were joking. Then she grinned. "Really? That's *fantastic*, girls. Go to the far side of the gym and wait for instructions. We'll get started soon."

"I love Ms. Pike," Alison said. "She's so cool."

"For a second, I thought she'd say no," I said.

Heather smirked. "Like we'd listen anyway."

We walked across the gym, bypassing the girls who'd picked up jump ropes and were practicing, and joined guys who had formed a line. I noticed Callie wasn't part of the lineup. Maybe she was skipping jump rope to cheer on Jacob instead.

"What're you doing?" Andy asked, walking over to us. I hadn't seen him around the stable much lately. Probably because he was Eric's friend and he was avoiding me.

Julia put her hands on her hips. "What does it look like we're doing?" she asked.

"Push-ups?" Andy asked slowly.

"Um, *yeah*," Alison said. "Jump rope is cool, but we're strong enough to hang with the boys."

Andy grinned and pushed back his light brown hair. "I like it. You're on."

He walked back to join the rest of the group who had decided to participate. I crossed my fingers that this was it.

But nope.

Ben, Julia's boyfriend, walked into the gym with Eric. Ben saw Julia and grinned. He was gorgeous—pale skin and dark hair. They'd been on the DL because Julia had been afraid Jasmine would try to break them up, but now they could be open about their relationship. By the way Ben was looking at Julia, it looked as if he was starting right now. I tensed, preparing myself for Eric to walk over to us with Ben, but he walked by and headed for the other guys. I let out a breath.

"Hey," Ben said, smiling at Julia. "I'm not even surprised."

I looked at him for a second, realizing he was lumping me in with the Trio. I'd never been part of a group, really. It had always been Paige and me or Callie and me. Never me and three other girls.

"Like we'd jump rope," Julia said. She flashed him a smile. "We're gonna take you down."

Ben squeezed Julia's hand. "I don't doubt it for a second."

Ms. Pike walked over and stopped in front of us. "It's time for the annual push-up contest. The rules are that you must do traditional push-ups and if your knees or stomach touch the floor, you're out. You also can't stop. You have to keep moving. Got it?"

We nodded.

"Physical competitions have occurred every Homecoming since this institution was started. I'm pleased to see you all here and participating. Go ahead and get ready," Ms. Pike said.

Just as we lowered ourselves to the ground, someone in red Converse sneakers walked by. I forced myself not to look up. I didn't need to see his face to know who it was. Jacob.

I could feel Heather looking over at me, but I ignored her gaze and kept my eyes on the gym floor. Someone else walked by and headed for the stands. I wondered if it was Callie, but I wasn't going to check to find out.

"And . . . ready, set, go!" Ms. Pike said.

I pushed up off the ground, then lowered myself back down. Up and down and up and down. I focused on breathing and not going too fast. But I also didn't go slow enough that Ms. Pike would eliminate me.

After five more push-ups, Alison flopped onto her

stomach. She rolled over onto her back, breathing hard. After a few seconds, she sat up and walked over to stand in front of us.

"C'mon, everyone!" she said. "Keep going!"

A few minutes later, a couple of guys dropped out and they joined Alison in cheering for their friends.

At the opposite end of the gym, other people were cheering for the girls jumping rope. I hoped Paige was doing well.

My arms burned and I felt beads of sweat forming on the back of my neck. I couldn't keep going much longer. I was surprised I'd managed to hang on this long. But maybe riding had built me up more than I'd thought. Outlasting some of the boys felt good!

"Ugh," Heather said, dropping to her knees. I looked at her out of the corner of my eye and her cheeks were pink. She got up and stood beside Alison.

I couldn't believe I'd beat Heather! Julia and I were the only girls left.

"I'm. Not. Going. To. Quit," Julia said, huffing.

"Me either," I said. I squeezed my eyes shut for a second and tried to ignore the searing pain in my arms and shoulders. I was almost done.

Andy joined the dropouts next.

My hands were starting to slip on the floor. I flicked my gaze over to Julia—she looked as if she could keep going for hours. There was no way. I couldn't—I dropped to my stomach.

Major. Ouch. Everything burned. I gulped air and tried to slow my crazy heartbeat. I felt as if I'd just run ten miles. I walked over and stood by Alison and Heather. Callie was sitting on the bleachers a few feet down, watching Jacob. He, Troy, Ben, Eric, and a few others were still going. I didn't let myself look at Eric or Jacob—I watched Julia.

Julia did two more push-ups, then lowered herself down. Her arms shook. Her face was red and her arms quivered as she tried to push herself back up.

"Go, Jules," Alison said. "You've got it!"

Julia made it halfway up and shook her head. She fell to her knees. "Oh. My. God," she said. "Pain."

Alison reached out and took Julia's hand, pulling her up.

"That was awesome," I said. "I would have died if I'd done one more."

Heather nodded at her. "Impressive."

We sat on the bottom row of the bleachers and watched the remaining guys do push-ups. One by one they dropped out. As I watched them quit, I knew what was going to happen before it did. A drop of sweat fell from Ben's fore-head to the floor and with a shake of his head, he got on his knees.

Eric and Jacob were the last two guys left that I knew.

"C'mon!" Ms. Pike said. "We're down to the final competitors. Who's going to win?"

Both of their faces were brilliant shades of red and their T-shirts were soaked.

Neither looked as if he was going to stop anytime soon. They both had the same look of determination on their faces.

"Go, Jacob!" Callie cheered.

"Yay, Eric!"

I looked past Callie and saw Rachel standing and clap-ping. I hadn't even seen her come in.

"C'mon, Eric!" Troy cheered.

"You've got it, Jacob," said one of the guys in our grade. "You're almost there, man."

I watched them both, knowing it would look bad if I got up and walked away. I tried to look at both of them, but I couldn't stop watching Jacob. *Go, go!* I cheered in my head. *You can do it!*

A crowd started to gather around them and everyone was cheering them on. The cheers seemed to give Jacob

and Eric a boost of energy and just when it looked as if their pace was starting to lag, they gained speed. The other guys looked as if they weren't going to stop, either.

Ms. Pike walked over. "Guys," she said. "You're all doing a wonderful job. You've got two minutes before I have to call a tie. Everyone has to get to class."

The crowd sighed, but I was glad. Knowing both guys and their history of hating each other—they'd keep going until they dropped.

Ms. Pike counted down the minutes and then everyone joined in for the final five seconds.

"Five, four, three, two, one!"

On one, Jacob and Eric looked at each other—a glare passing between them—and they both got to their feet. Jacob's light brown hair was a little sweaty and his green eyes darkened after looking at Eric.

"Congratulations, Eric and Jacob," Ms. Pike said. "That was fantastic. You both displayed a tremendous amount of strength and drive. I don't know if we've ever had the competition last this long!"

Neither guy looked at each other—they just moved a few steps away.

Rachel bounced over to Eric and smiled up at him. "You were *so* awesome," she said.

"Thanks," Eric said, trying to regain his breath.

Callie walked up to Jacob and reached out to hug him. Jacob stiffened and he leaned his body away from Callie's and gave her an awkward one-armed hug. Callie pulled away from him, frowning.

"I don't want to get you all gross," he explained.

"Oh," she said, nodding. "Right. But you were amazing. You didn't even have to keep going—I know you would have won."

Jacob's eyes connected with mine over the top of Callie's head.

I looked away and got up from the bleachers.

"I have to see how Paige did," I said to the Trio. They nodded and I headed to the opposite side of the gym. Another gym teacher was telling the remaining jump ropers that it was time to stop and get ready for class. Paige and Geena were jumping side by side and they jumped a couple more times before stopping.

"That was great," I said, smiling at both of them.

"Thanks," Paige said. Her cheeks were pink and she and Geena caught their breaths. "You were awesome, too. I thought you were really going to take down the boys."

"I definitely tried, but there was no way I could have

won," I said, grinning. "Maybe I *do* need to start taking gym."

Paige and Geena laughed and the three of us walked out of the gym together.

When I walked into the theater for class, I looked for Heather, but I'd beat her here and Jacob was already onstage. Ms. Scott smiled at me as I put my bag on my seat.

"Go ahead onstage, Sasha," she said. "We're going to do an exercise before we start our lesson."

"Okay," I said.

I walked up the stairs and tried to keep my ballet flats from making a sound as I walked onstage and stood behind a couple of girls in my class. I wanted to blend in with them and I hoped Jacob would stay where he was and not come over and talk to me.

"Hey, Sash," said Whitney, a black-haired girl with cute, blunt-cut bangs.

"Hey," I said.

Her friend, Aprilynne, smiled at me. "So, are you freaking out about Homecoming?" she asked.

I faked a smile. "Oh, totally. I'm definitely freaking out about it."

Just not in the way they thought.

Whitney brushed her bangs out of her face. "I'm going solo, but there's this guy that I'm in looove with in my history class. I hope he asks me."

"Who?" Aprilynne asked. "I didn't know you liked someone!"

Whitney smiled. "Carter. He picked up my pen when I dropped it yesterday and we shared my book because he forgot his."

"Omigod," Aprilynne said. "That's so cute!"

I looked past them as they chattered about Homecoming. Jacob was still talking to one of the guys in class. Whew. Aprilynne and Whitney's convo about Homecoming wasn't the ideal conversation, but at least Jacob wasn't trying to talk to me.

"Seriously?" someone said in my ear.

I jumped and turned around to see Heather.

"What?" I asked.

She gave me a knowing look. I smiled at Whitney and Aprilynne and drifted off to the side of the stage with Heather.

"You were subjecting yourself to *that* conversation of 'omigod-Carter's-so-cute-and-I-looove-Homecoming' for what reason?"

"I didn't want Jacob to talk to me," I said. Why had I suddenly become so honest with Heather? Probably because she was the only person who really knew what was going on, and I had to tell her the truth or she'd call me on it.

"Then you're going to learn how to say 'Jacob, I'm not talking to you right now,'" Heather said. "Otherwise, you'll be stuck hiding with two girls who won't talk about anything but your fave topic."

I sighed. "Yeah, I know. That was lame."

"Yeah, it was." Heather shook her head, laughing.

I rolled my eyes at her, but didn't want her to go. Luckily, Ms. Scott moved to the front of the stage and looked up at us, ending my convo with Heather.

"Hi, class," Ms. Scott said. "Today, we're going to play a quick game called Blob. It's going to teach you how to work together and use each other. Here's how we play: Aidan, you're 'it.' You're the blob."

Aidan laughed. "Cool."

"Everyone else needs to avoid Aidan because he's going to try to tag you," Ms. Scott said. "When he does, you need to stay attached to him since you're now part of the blob. You have to work together to tag someone else. The blob will grow and as more people are tagged, it will require more teamwork on your part to move cohesively and tag people."

We all nodded. This sounded fun.

"This is a great game to build trust with your fellow actors and to understand that you must learn how to take direction in theater. Questions?" Ms. Scott asked.

No one had any. We were ready.

"Aidan, move up to the front of the stage and give everyone a second to find a spot," Ms. Scott said.

Aidan walked to the front of the stage and brushed back his light brown hair. He grinned at us. "I'm taking all of you down," he said.

"Good luck!" Whitney called, laughing.

Aidan made a face at us and fake-braced himself like a runner getting ready to sprint.

"Get ready and . . . go!" Ms. Scott said.

Aidan started to lunge to the right, but changed directions midstep and dashed in the other direction. Everyone scattered and a couple of girls screamed as he ran at them. He touched Lexa's shoulder and she grabbed his elbow with one hand, joining him. He tried to run to tag Whitney, but Lexa went after Jacob. Aidan tugged her in his direction and she laughed as she almost fell over.

"Aidan!" Lexa said.

"Sorry," he said, grinning.

"Figure out how to work together, class," Ms. Scott said.

Aiden whispered in Lexa's ear and they both ran to the right side of the stage and chased Aprilynne.

"Lexa!" Aprilynne said when her friend tapped her arm.

Lexa grinned and grabbed Aprilynne's hand. Together, Aidan, Lexa, and Aprilynne walked back across the stage, faked a right and then tagged a guy in the class. I tried to stay in the back of the middle of the stage. I didn't want to get trapped in a corner.

The blob kept growing as more people got tagged. The group snagged Heather next and she looped her arm through Whitney's. The group lunged at me and, laughing, I tried to dodge them, but Heather's fingertip touched my shoulder blade.

"Gotcha, Silver," Heather said, smirking.

"Yeah, whatever," I said, fake-grumbling. I linked arms with her and Aidan motioned for us to huddle up.

"Three people left," he said. "We need to pretend we're going after Derek, but get Jacob. He'll have nowhere to go or he'll fall off the stage."

Um, *no*! We couldn't go after Jacob yet or he'd be attached to me. That could not happen!

"I think Derek's an easier target," I said.

"Aidan's right," Heather said, not looking at me. "We need to grab Jacob. He's had it pretty easy this whole time. No one wanted to go after him 'cause he's on the track team. Let's get him."

Everyone nodded and it was done—no one had listened to me. Since I was attached to Heather, I knew throwing it wasn't an option. She was ultracompetitive and she'd kill me if I purposely messed it up.

We started walking toward Derek and he shifted from foot to foot, ready to run away from us. Just as we got within feet of him, we ran sideways and caught Jacob by surprise. He jumped to the side, trying to avoid us, but Aidan was too quick. He touched Jacob's arm and, smiling, Jacob shook his head.

"So close," he said.

He walked around the group and stood beside me.

"Um," he said, starting to reach for my arm.

"Uh," I said. Two-letter words were obviously our mode of communication. "Go ahead."

He linked his arm through mine loose enough that we were barely touching. But it was enough to almost make me forget how to walk. What if Callie came in and saw us? Neither of us had planned it, obviously, but I didn't want her to see us this close. Even for a game.

But I couldn't think about it anymore as the group moved forward and tagged Derek, leaving Vanessa as the winner.

I detangled myself from Heather and Jacob, glad the game was over.

"That was great, everyone," Ms. Scott said. "You all learned to move together even though it got more difficult as you added people. I was impressed with your ability to work together as a group. Nice job." She smiled at us. "Okay, now that we're all warmed up, please take your seats."

Those were four words I needed to hear.

5

THREE RIDERS,
ONE SEAT,

LATER THAT AFTERNOON I WALKED DOWN the main aisle of the stable and headed for the tack room. My mind was focused on only one thing—the tape for Mr. Nicholson. Even though Jas was gone, it didn't matter. My riding skills were going to be compared to Heather's. As if that wasn't enough, both of our rides were being held up against everyone else who rode for the YENT at different schools across the country. My stomach flipped at the thought.

"Don't tack up yet," someone called.

I looked back and Heather motioned to me. "Mr. Conner wants us in his office first."

I walked over to Heather. "Probably about Julia and Alison."

"Prob," Heather said. "All I want is to hear him say that they're back on the team."

We walked to his office together and Heather knocked on the door.

"Come in," he said.

Heather walked inside and I followed her.

Mr. Conner was sitting behind his giant wooden desk. It was covered in papers and stacks of files.

"Take a seat," he said.

Heather and I sat in the comfy office chairs across from him. I clenched my fingers together. I wanted to hear whatever he had to say, but I was also ready to start the lesson and do the tape for Mr. Nicholson.

Mr. Conner closed a file on his desk and cleared his throat. "As I'm sure you're already aware," he said. "Jasmine has been expelled from Canterwood Crest. In addition, we have discovered proof that Julia and Alison did not cheat on their exam."

Mr. Conner ran a hand over his short black hair. "I'm sorry this happened to Alison and Julia. They missed their chance at the YENT. I regret their innocence wasn't proven earlier."

Heather shifted in her seat and Mr. Conner looked at her. "I apologize for not taking your claims about their innocence more seriously," he said. "You have to under-stand that we thought the cheat sheets were real."

Heather nodded. "I know. I'm just glad that everyone knows they didn't cheat."

"They will also be immediately reinstated on the advanced team," Mr. Conner said.

Heather and I smiled at each other.

"I've also spoken with Mr. Nicholson this morning," Mr. Conner continued. "He's agreed to hold another tryout for the YENT the week after fall break. So those who qualified for testing last time, Julia, Callie, and Alison, will have the opportunity to try out for Jasmine's seat."

Endless possibilities started running through my brain. Callie deserved to make the YENT. After all, it was partly my fault—and Jacob's—that she didn't make it the first time. But if Callie did make the team, it would be *so* uncomfortable. She hated me and lessons would be the worst if she made it. Alison and Julia were excellent riders, too, and they also deserved it. I hated wanting someone other than Callie to make the team, but I also had to get the most out of my lessons. And I didn't know if I could do that with Callie in the arena with me.

"Julia and Alison will resume lessons tomorrow," Mr. Conner said. "I'm thrilled to have them back on the advanced team."

He nodded once at us. "If you don't have any questions, then go tack up your horses and I'll see you in the indoor arena."

Heather and I stood and left his office.

"It's going to start all over again," Heather said as we walked to the tack room.

I pushed open the door. "What?"

"The craziness over the YENT. Mr. Conner must have just finished that phone call. If Julia and Alison knew about the YENT tryouts, they would have already told me."

"He's probably calling to tell them now," I said. I walked past rows of gleaming saddles, taking in the smell of leather. "They're going to freak."

Heather slid Aristocrat's saddle over her arm and hung his bridle over her shoulder. "And so is Callie."

I played with Charm's snaffle bit. "Three riders."

"One seat," Heather finished.

6

THAT RED LIGHT

I FELT DIZZY AS I TACKED UP CHARM. MY fingers kept slipping as I tried to run down his stirrup leathers and my hands shook as I slid the bit into his mouth and bridled him. Charm was always able to sense my mood. He nudged my arm with his muzzle. I looked into his big brown eyes.

"Thanks, boy," I said, hugging his neck. "I know *you're* going to do great. I just need to relax."

My phone buzzed on my wooden tack trunk and I walked around Charm to check it.

Good luck! U r going 2 kill it! <3

Paige.

Thx! Hope so!! I wrote back.

I put on my black helmet and took Charm's reins,

scanning him one last time to make sure he looked perfect for Mr. Nicholson. His chestnut coat gleamed, his blaze and sock were clean, and I'd painted his hooves with clear polish. He was so ready. I looked down at my own blue button-down shirt and tan breeches to make sure I was as spotless as Charm.

"That's as good as you're going to look, so let's go already," Heather said. She walked past Charm and me, leading Aristocrat. The darker chestnut Thoroughbred laid back his ears a fraction as he passed Charm. The two had been rivals since our first day at Canterwood.

"Wow, thanks," I said, but I followed Heather and Aristocrat down the aisle and we made our way toward the indoor arena.

I watched Heather and she acted as if she could do this every day.

We reached the indoor arena and mounted once we'd led the horses through the entrance. I walked Charm in the opposite direction of Aristocrat and started warming him up along the wall. Charm, a Thoroughbred/Belgian mix, didn't want to walk for long. He loved to move fast and within minutes, he was tugging on the reins and asking to trot.

I gave him rein and he moved into a smooth trot, his

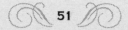

long strides quickly covering the arena ground. The dirt muffled the sounds of his shoes and we made a couple of circles around the far side of the arena and left the other end for Heather and Aristocrat. *Just pretend it's any other warm-up*, I told myself. No big deal.

We changed directions and made a few more circles before Mr. Conner came into the arena. Heather and I slowed our horses and lined them up in front of him.

I started breathing faster, knowing I couldn't trick myself into forgetting that the camera was on. This *wasn't* any other warm-up. It was the first time Mr. Nicholson would see our riding since YENT camp. He could decide that I hadn't improved or . . . had gotten worse and remove me from the team. The thought was enough to make me nauseous.

"Hi, girls," Mr. Conner said. "I hope you're ready to get started." He tipped his head in the direction of the camera. "I'm going to turn on the camera and then we'll begin. This will be a normal lesson, so there's no reason to be nervous. All right?"

We nodded.

Mr. Conner walked to the camera and tripod and pushed a button. A tiny red light went on. That light had sealed Jas's fate and it was about to do the same for me.

"Please walk your horses to the wall," Mr. Conner

called. He moved to the center of the arena and held his clipboard in front of him.

I pushed my heels down and sat deep in the saddle. Charm walked toward the wall and we passed the window that overlooked the big pasture with the rolling hill. As soon as the test was over, I'd cool Charm and turn him out. He'd need a break after this.

"Trot," Mr. Conner called.

I gave Charm rein and he moved into a smooth, easy trot. Ahead of us, Heather posted to Aristocrat's trot and the two were in perfect unison. I directed my attention back to Charm and ignored Heather and Aristocrat. I couldn't lose focus for a second.

"Reverse directions and sitting trot," Mr. Conner said. As Charm and I changed directions, I saw him scribble something on his black clipboard. For a second, I wondered if he was writing about something I'd done wrong. Or maybe it was about Heather.

Stop it! I yelled to myself. Whenever I'd lost focus before, I'd always messed up. That wasn't happening again.

I took a breath and regained my attention. At least Heather was behind us now and I couldn't watch her.

"Halt," Mr. Conner said. In three strides, I'd brought Charm to a stop.

"Trot halfway around the arena, then canter," Mr. Conner said.

I urged Charm into a trot and posted until we reached the halfway point of the arena. I gave him rein and sat in the saddle, letting him move into a canter. Charm shook out his mane and leaped forward, a little too fast, and I jolted backward a bit. I fought to keep my face from turning red as I righted my body in the saddle.

You should have been prepared for that, I told myself.

I eased Charm's canter a bit and he flicked his tail, annoyed at being told to slow down. But he listened and didn't fight me.

"Slow to a trot and begin figure eights," Mr. Conner said.

Charm slowed and we began the pattern. After a few figure eights, Mr. Conner asked us to walk the horses for a couple of minutes. Then, he made us do spirals.

"All right," he said, holding up a hand. "Stop and walk your horses to the other end of the arena. You'll take a few jumps and when you're both finished, you may cool out your horses."

I almost wanted to shout, *YES!* I'd been worried that this would be the lesson Mr. Conner would make us do dressage instead of jumping. Dressage wasn't my strongest

area and even though Charm and I were working on it, I wanted Mr. Nicholson to see us jump. Charm's first love was cross-country, but he was great at indoor courses too.

"Heather, please start when you're ready," Mr. Conner said.

Heather circled Aristocrat twice and I watched as she quieted him with her hands and legs before pointing him toward the first jump. The course had a tall vertical, a double combination, a shorter vertical, and then an oxer. I already knew the combination would be the trickiest for Charm and me. Sometimes, he got excited and tried to rush fences. With the combo, he couldn't do that. Eyeing the double, I knew Charm only had two strides before we had to take off from the first half of the combination to the second. It was going to be tight.

Heather's blond hair, wavy today, flowed out from under her helmet as Aristocrat cantered toward the first jump. At just the right moment, Heather rose into the two-point position and kneaded her hands along Aristocrat's neck. The gelding jumped into the air, tucking his forelegs under his body. He cleared the vertical and they headed for the combo. Heather's timing was perfect as she let him go and he leaped the first half of the combination, then cantered for two strides before lifting into the air for the second half. They made everything look easy, but I knew how hard Heather had worked to get here.

The short vertical and oxer weren't a problem for Aristocrat or Heather. They cleared them easily and Aristocrat tossed his head as Heather cantered him away from the course. He knew he'd done well and he acted as if he wanted to go again.

My fingers started to grip the reins, but I made myself relax. If I tensed, so would Charm, and I wanted him to be cool through the course.

Like Heather with Aristocrat, I moved Charm through two circles before guiding him toward the red and white vertical. We flew into the air with perfect timing and he landed with a quiet thud on the other side. The first half of the combination loomed in front of us. Charm snorted and asked for more rein, but I held him back. If he gathered too much speed, it would be hard to slow him enough through the double.

Charm lifted into the air for the first half of the combo and I rose slightly out of the saddle. I kept my heels pushed down and my hands steady along Charm's neck. He landed on the other side my heartbeat seemed to echo in my ears as loud as Charm's hoofbeats.

Two. . . one. . . now! I counted the strides between the halves of the combo and urged Charm into the air. He snapped his knees sharply under his body and arched over the jump. That was my favorite feeling—being suspended in the air for the briefest second. Charm hit the ground and we moved to the short vertical. Charm's ears pricked forward and he jumped it eagerly and applied the same enthusiasm to the oxer.

"Good boy," I said, trying not to dance in the saddle. Instead, I patted his neck. He'd done a great job and we couldn't have had a better ride. As he slowed to a trot, the stress of worrying about the tape started to melt away. I'd been worried about it for forever and now it was done.

I rode Charm next to Aristocrat and stopped him. Heather looked over at me and gave me a nod.

"Not a disaster," she said, her tone light. "I mean, you didn't fall off or anything."

"Thanks a lot."

Mr. Conner finished writing on his clipboard and smiled at both of us.

"Those were excellent rides, girls," he said. "Please dismount and cool your horses. See you next class."

He shut off the camera and I dismounted. When my feet hit the ground, I felt all of the tension that been building for days start to drain from my body. It was a mixture of relief that the tape was over and exhaustion from worrying about it so much. I leaned lightly against Charm's shoulder and for what felt like the first time in a while, I took a breath.

7

HOMECOMING THREW UP ALL OVER CAMPUS

HEATHER AND I COOLED THE HORSES WITHOUT saying a word to each other. I had a feeling she had been as nervous as I'd been about the test, but she'd never admit it. I clipped Charm into crossties and groomed him. He was so shiny from when I'd prepared him for the tape that all he needed was a light body brush.

I unclipped the crossties and led him down the aisle. "You deserve to spend the night outside in the big pasture, boy," I said. He followed me outside and we walked across the stable yard to the pasture. We passed the outdoor arena where Callie was riding by herself. I paused, unable to look away. Black Jack, Callie's Morab gelding, was flexing his leg and back as Callie took him at an extended trot around the arena. His shiny black coat caught the sunlight and he looked gorgeous.

I turned away and caught Charm watching them too. His head was raised high so he could see and his eyes were on Jack. Unlike Callie and me, they were still BFFs.

"C'mon, boy," I said. I tugged gently on his lead line and opened the gate to the pasture. I walked him inside, then unclipped his lead line. He stood beside me, not moving. I sighed and wrapped my arms around his neck. "I get it. I miss them too." I dropped down and sat cross-legged in the grass. I plucked a blade of grass and twirled it in my fingers. Charm lowered his head and started grazing near me. I kept my back to Callie and just listened to the sound of Jack's hoofbeats in the arena.

When I left the pasture, the sky was starting to turn pink, orange, and purple. I hadn't realized how long I'd stayed with Charm. I walked through the center of campus and fought the urge to shield my eyes. It looked like Homecoming had thrown up all over campus and it kept multiplying every day. This morning five or six yard signs had been stuck along the sidewalk that I took from the courtyard to Winchester. Now, a dozen signs on either side of the sidewalk directed students to Homecoming activities and promoted the week's contests. Every dorm hall had a banner over their entrance and I looked down so

I didn't have to see the WINCHESTER 4 THE WIN! sign that draped over our entrance.

Inside the dorm I hurried down the hallway to my room. If I saw one more inch of green or gold . . . . I paused outside my dorm and took a breath. Paige had decorated the white board outside our door with a green marker. Her fun, flirty script read *Sasha & Paige <3 Homecoming! Go CC!*

I rubbed my eyes for a second, then opened the door. Paige was at her desk, typing on her laptop. She had her stack of textbooks beside her and her bio notebook was open. Maybe now was the perfect time to tell her what really had happened at my party.

"How's the homework?" I asked.

Paige looked up from her computer. "Almost done. One more question to answer. How was your taping? I was going to text you, but I figured you were probably decompressing with Charm."

"You know me so well," I said. "The taping went great, actually, and I was hanging with Charm in the pasture. He did a fantastic job."

Paige beamed. "See? Told you there was nothing to worry about."

"I was sooo nervous, but we got through it. And at

least I'm so busy that I don't have much time to worry about what Mr. Nicholson is going to say about how I rode."

"From what you just told me," Paige said. "I don't think you have anything to worry about."

I grabbed a clean T-shirt and yoga pants, heading to the shower.

"I'm going to meet Ryan at the Sweet Shoppe as soon as I finish my homework," Paige said. "You want to come? It's going to be *awesome*. I heard that all of the treats are green and gold!"

Siiigh. Talking to Paige wasn't going to happen now.

"That sounds like so much fun," I said. "But I've got homework."

I left out the part that I couldn't stand one more second of Homecoming.

"Okay," Paige said. "Totally get it. I'll bring you back something fun. I heard they have cookies with green and specially made gold M&M's."

"Cool. Have fun with Ryan."

"I will. I can't wait."

Paige went back to her homework and I headed to the shower. I took extra time shampooing my hair—I wanted to make sure Paige was gone before I came out. I dressed, dried my hair, and took longer than usual to flatiron it. I eased open the bathroom door, afraid Paige was still here. But our room was empty.

I hated that things were off between Paige and me, but I just couldn't deal with the Homecoming talk. I didn't want to take anything away from Paige's excitement, but it just annoyed me.

I unpacked my books from my bag got ready to do homework. It was surprisingly light for tonight. I settled on my bed and started on my math homework. Right now, it was one of the few times I wished I could go back home for the night—or the week. Canterwood was the last place I wanted to be right now. I knew exactly how tonight would go: Paige would come back and gush about her date with Ryan and that *was* something I wanted to hear about. I loved seeing her excited about a guy and it was fun to analyze every minute of her dates. But the topic of conversation would eventually switch over to Homecoming. And it was wearing on me. Fast.

8

YOU IN?

AN HOUR LATER, I WAS ABOUT TO TAKE A break when my phone beeped. I flipped it open and found a text from Heather. *Come over 4 a sec.*

What's up? I texted back.

OMG, if ur gonna ask 20 ?s 4get it.

Sry, jeez. B rite over.

I was too intrigued to pass up a visit to the Trio's suite. Heather never asked me over just because. There was always a reason.

I slid on silver flip-flops, applied a quick coat of orange-strawberry gloss, and grabbed my purse.

When I got to Orchard, I hurried to their room— eager to get inside and minimize any chance of seeing Callie. I knocked on the door and Julia let me in. She actually smiled at me. It was a nice change from the usual look of disgust on her face when she saw me. But I wondered how long she'd be nice to me before she went back to Old Julia.

"Hey," Alison said, walking out of her room. She looked cozy-chic in a white cotton sundress with a half dozen plastic bangles on her wrist.

"Heather's got something to show you in her room," Julia said.

I followed them into Heather's room and she turned to look at us, shaking her head at me. "It took you, like, forever to get here, Silver. Don't get lost next time."

"I didn't get lost," I said. "And I got here in five minutes."

Heather dismissed me with a wave of her hand. "Whatever. Anyway, since you're finally here, we can talk about tomorrow's Homecoming sitch. It's, *gag*, Crazy Dress Day."

I nodded, but was totally unsure what this had to do with anything. Julia and Alison sat at the edge of Heather's bed and I leaned against the doorjamb.

"I'm sure you've already come up with a *fantastic*, brilliant idea for an outfit," Heather said, her tone oozing sarcasm. "But since we all know you haven't, I've obviously come up with a solution."

Heather pulled open her closet door and reached inside. She pulled out an outfit and held it up. "Interested?"

All I could do was stare. It was a crisp show shirt, red jacket, and ivory breeches. These were show clothes I'd drooled over in catalogs but couldn't afford.

"Oh, and these," Heather said. She leaned down and grabbed a pair of tall black boots. She set them in front of me and I almost stopped breathing. They were Cavallo boots. Fifteen-hundred-dollar Cavallo boots. I had to force myself not to reach down to pet them.

"Heather, that outfit's gorgeous," I said. "Wow. But it's probably too small for me." I wasn't willowy like her.

Heather snorted. "Puh-lease. I live in Manhattan. I knew your size two seconds after I met you. Everything will fit. We're all wearing our best show clothes. You in?"

I hesitated. If I took the clothes, what did that mean? *Oh stop it,* I told myself. It meant nothing. They weren't inviting me into their group—all they were doing was offering to let me dress up with them.

"Silver? Hello?" Heather said.

"Okay," I said, smiling. "We're going to have the coolest outfits."

Alison tossed her hair over her shoulder. "Of course we are. And everyone else can be jealous of us."

"As if they ever aren't," Julia said with a smirk.

Heather handed me the clothes and boots. "These better come back in the same condition that I gave them to you or you'll have to sell Charm to pay me back."

"I'll be careful with them." But I was already wondering if I should really take the expensive clothes and boots.

Heather shook her head. "Oh my God, take them and go. I was just kidding."

"Okay, thanks. I've got to go anyway and get back to my homework."

"I've got a ton of homework too," Alison said. "Ugh."

"See you," Julia said. With a smile, I left them and walked out of Heather's bedroom. I let myself out of their suite, carrying Heather's clothes and boots. I wasn't becoming part of the *Trio*, was I?

9

A SURPRISE . . .
FOR PAIGE

YAWNING, I DRAGGED MYSELF OUT OF BED on Tuesday morning and Paige bounded up to me.

"Hi!" she said, her voice way too high for this time in the morning. She looked as if she'd been up for hours.

I rubbed my eyes. "Did you have chocolate-covered espresso beans or something?"

Paige shook her head. "Nope! I just have a surprise for you."

That made me wake up a little more. "Ooh, a surprise. Tell me!"

Paige turned toward her clothes and looked back over her shoulder at me. "I have to show you. Close your eyes."

I sat at the end of my bed and closed them. I heard Paige shuffle through her closet, then there was silence.

"All right," she said. "Open!"

I did and Paige stood in front of me, beaming, and holding out two outfits on purple hangers.

"I'm going to be a chef and you're my sous chef!" Paige said, grinning. "Isn't that awesome? The white one's mine and yours is the black."

Paige's outfit had a jacket, chef's hat, and pants. Mine had a jacket, pants, and an apron. I chewed on my lower lip and tried to think of what to say. Paige had gotten the outfits and she was so excited. Plus, it was a fab idea since idea since she hosted *Teen Cuisine*, a cooking show on The Food Network for Kids.

"What's wrong?" she asked. She hung the clothes on her closet doorknob. "If you don't like it, we can totally do something else. I should have asked you what you wanted to do, but I thought this would be a fun surprise."

"It is," I said. "The outfits are so perfect. But . . ." I got off my bed and walked to my own closet.

"But what?" Paige asked.

"I went over to the Trio's when you were out with Ryan. Heather asked me to come over and said she had something for me."

I reached into my closet and pulled out the clothes and boots from Heather.

Paige tilted her head. "Heather's letting you borrow those clothes? Wow—aren't those boots you'd wear to a big show?"

"Yeah, they are. But she didn't give me the clothes for a show. She gave me clothes for . . . today."

"Today?" Paige repeated.

"The Trio asked me to dress up with them last night. If I'd known you'd already had an outfit planned, I never would have said yes."

"I was going to tell you, but I thought it would be a better surprise," Paige said. "I didn't think anyone else would ask you to dress up with them."

For a second, that sort of stung. She made it sound as if I didn't have other friends. But I knew Paige hadn't meant it that way. And she had every right to think that, anyway—I *had* no other friends—definitely not the Trio.

"It doesn't matter what I told the Trio," I said. "I'll text Heather and tell her I'm dressing up with you instead. I'd rather match with you anyway."

I put the clothes on my bed and reached for my phone.

"Don't," Paige said. "You already told them yes. I should have told you earlier. I'll text one of my other friends or I'll just dress up by myself. No big deal."

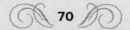

But it was a big deal to Paige. I could see it through her forced smile.

"You sure?" I asked. "I'm serious. I can tell them no."

"Totally sure," Paige said. "Go with the Trio."

She walked away from me and into the bathroom, closing the door behind her.

I picked up my phone and started a new text. The right thing to do was to dress up with Paige—my best friend. Not the Trio.

Sry, but I'm dressing up w/Paige.

I went to press send, but my finger hovered over the button. I hit cancel instead and snapped my phone shut. The Trio was going to be a Quartet today.

Paige and I didn't say much to each other as we got ready and left for class. We stayed out of each other's way, easing past each other to go back and forth from the bedroom to the bathroom as we hurried to get dressed and do our hair and makeup. It was the first time Paige and I had split on an activity we'd usually do together.

"You look great," I said.

"You too," Paige said. She gave me a half smile and we left our room for the cafeteria. We got inside and started for the breakfast line.

"I'm thinking waffles," I said. "You?"

"Hmm. Maybe pancakes," Paige said. "Or—" She stopped and I looked at her.

"What?"

Paige jerked her head in the direction of the tables. "Nothing. Just looks like someone wants you to sit with them."

I glanced over and Alison waved at me, motioning for me to come over.

I waved back and turned to Paige. "It's fine. I'll still sit with you. We can talk—we never have time anymore."

Paige reached the stack of trays and grabbed one. "Actually, I can't talk right now. Geena and I have to go over verrry last-minute details for the dance. It's totally cool if you sit with them."

"Oh," I said, taking my own tray. "Okay."

Homecoming. Again.

Paige and I got our breakfasts and separated.

"Sasha!" Alison said. She hopped out of her chair to stand by me. "Omigod, we look awesome!" Alison waved her hands up and down, motioning at her own outfit. She'd dressed in black breeches with suede knees, a white show shirt, and a navy jacket.

"We totally do," I said, smiling. But it faded quickly when I thought about Paige.

"What's wrong with you so early?" Heather asked, squinting at me.

"Homecoming," I grumbled. "At least I can sit here and not have to listen to Paige and Geena debate if the plates should be green and gold, green, or just gold."

Alison shook her head. "Sasha, Sasha. That's a VIP decision. We're going to remember that night for the rest of our lives and if the plates are wrong . . ."

My eyes met Heather's and we shared a semitortured look.

"If anyone even *thinks* the word 'Homecoming' during breakfast," Heather said. "You're eating alone."

I grinned and poured maple syrup onto my waffle, certain I wouldn't hear a mention of Homecoming for the next half hour.

After breakfast I met up with Paige in the hallway on our way to class. We exchanged smiles, but that was it. We walked to Mr. Davidson's English class together, but the walk, which usually felt short because we chatted the entire way, seemed to take forever. Our silence felt even more noticeable because everyone around us was energized about Homecoming. It looked as though every student had taken advantage of crazy dress day—it was like Halloween. I couldn't help but stare when Rachel and her friends walked by in striped knee socks and shorts. I wondered if Eric knew that she was dressing up. I almost stopped walking as I envisioned Eric seeing Rachel's outfit and telling her how great it was and how much he liked it. I wanted that attention, too, but . . . from Jacob.

"Look at that," Paige said, jolting me out of my thoughts.

A guy with mismatched shoes headed up the steps to the science building.

Paige and I entered the English building and walked into Mr. Davidson's classroom.

"Hey," Alison said to Paige and me, walking over. She waved at both of us. "Aren't these outfits great?"

"They're fab," Paige said, stepping around us and taking her seat.

I sat next to Paige. That your-outfits-are-so-fab line was just that—a line.

"I *love* your outfit, too, Paige," Alison said. "It's genius because of the whole *Teen Cuisine* thing."

"Thanks," Paige said. Her tone was clipped and she didn't even look up at Alison. She leaned down and pulled her book and notebook out of her bag.

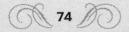

"We'll have to get a pic of you in your outfit," I said. "Maybe the show will want to share it with viewers."

"Yeah, maybe," Paige said. She looked away from me and it was clear she wasn't going to say anything else.

Ugh. I couldn't have her be mad at me too. It was too much on top of everything else that was going on. I tried to think of something to say that would make Paige feel better.

"So, for lunch," I said. "I was thinking we could grab our food and eat it outside because it's so nice. Want to?"

Paige looked over at me. "That sounds fun. I'd like that." She smiled, this time for real. It had been a while since we'd had lunch together. I'd been sitting with the Trio a lot and Paige had been with her friends. I settled back into my chair and breathed a sigh of relief. I couldn't lose the last real friend I had.

When I finally met Paige for lunch, she was back to her bubbly self. We loaded our trays with spaghetti, salad, and breadsticks. We filled cups with soda and carried our trays to a bench just outside the caf.

"Omigod," Paige said. "I can't believe it's already Tuesday! That means tomorrow's Wednesday." Paige pouted.

"What's wrong with Wednesday?" I asked. I swirled my fork in my spaghetti, then put it down. I stuck a napkin in my collar, knowing I looked like a giant dork. But that was better than getting spaghetti sauce on Heather's shirt and facing certain death.

"Sasha!" Paige turned to face me and almost knocked her tray off her lap. "Because! It's the middle of the week and that means Homecoming is half over!"

Paige's tone rose with every word—it was like she was spewing exclamation points.

"Oh, yeah," I said, trying to sound sorry. "That."

"I just can't wait for Green-and-Gold Day on Thursday, and then Friday's the dance. I'm going to be going *crazy* on Thursday. I want to deep condition my hair, do my nails . . ."

I had to tune out Paige's chatter about Homecoming. Instead, I thought about riding and concentrated on not spilling anything on Heather's clothes. For the rest of lunch, I just nodded and pretended to listen.

After my last class of the day, I walked down the hallway of the math building. I was sooo ready for my riding lesson. I half-wanted to skip changing into my riding clothes, but I knew Heather would kill me if I rode in hers. I was almost to the door when I saw Callie and Jacob walking in front of me.

Callie reached over to touch his upper arm and he moved a step away from her to shift his backpack from one shoulder to the other. He kept the distance between himself and Callie. She glanced down at her feet and stayed just behind him as they walked to the door. He pushed open the door and let her walk in front of him.

That was weird.

Why was Jacob being strange around her? He'd promised he'd never spill our secret about what had really happened between us, and I believed him, but what I'd just seen made me worry. *It's probably nothing,* I told myself. I had to believe that or I'd make myself crazy.

10

THE LAST PERSON
I WANT TO TALK TO

I RUSHED THROUGH GETTING DRESSED AND hurried to the stable, determined to spend as much time there as possible. I needed some serious Charm time and I was going to give him an extra-special grooming.

"Hi, guy," I said to Charm as I walked toward him. He had his head stuck over the stall door and his big brown eyes watched me approach.

I kissed his cheek and reached into my back pocket. "I *might* have brought you something from the common room kitchen," I said. "Something you might want."

I had Charm's full attention. He stretched his neck over the stall door, watching me reach into my back pocket.

I pulled out half a carrot and held it up, grinning at him. "Does this interest you?"

Charm bobbed his head and strained to reach the carrot.

"Aw, here, boy."

I flattened my hand and put the carrot on my palm. I held it out to Charm and he almost inhaled it. While he chomped on it, I took out his tack box from the trunk outside his stall and took his lead line off the hook.

I went into his stall and clipped the lead line under his chin. We walked out into the aisle together and I found a free pair of crossties.

"Let's make you sparkly and shiny," I said.

I rummaged through Charm's tack box for his body brush and laughed as he pawed the aisle floor with his right foreleg.

"Feeling extra good today? It was the carrot, huh," I said.

I ran the brush lightly over his body—he hadn't gotten dirty since yesterday's grooming. After just minutes, his coat was new-penny bright and his sock was stark white. I combed his mane, tail, and forelock. They detangled easily and I inspected Charm's bridle path and whiskers.

"It's going to be trim time for you soon," I said. "We'll have to get out the clippers."

Charm wouldn't mind that. The buzz of the clippers

never bothered him—he loved any kind of attention. After I wiped his eyes and muzzle with a damp cloth, I tacked him up and put on my helmet.

Mike walked down the aisle toward us and smiled at me.

"Mr. Conner wants you to meet in the stable yard," Mike said. Charm stretched his neck toward his favorite groom.

"Okay, thanks," I said. I led Charm past him. Just outside of the stable exit, Heather and Aristocrat were waiting.

"Hey," Heather said, giving me a half smile.

I mounted and rode Charm next to her. "Cross-country, maybe?" I asked.

Heather shrugged. "Maybe. Either that or practicing in the arena. But we haven't done cross-country in a while."

We grinned simultaneously when we saw Mr. Conner leaving the stable—on horseback. He trotted Lexington, a sweet gray gelding that he was training, in our direction. Mr. Conner didn't have much time to ride and when he did, it was to train horses—not ride with us. He was carrying a stack of something, but I couldn't see what they were. Then they came into focus.

"Cross-country vests!" I whispered.

"Hi, girls," Mr. Conner said, drawing Lexington to a smooth halt. "We're going to work on cross-country today. I thought we'd take a new course through the back woods and since it's different, I'll lead the way. Sound good?"

"Yes!" Heather and I said in unison.

Mr. Conner smiled. "Good. We won't be taking a ridiculous amount of jumps, but rather focusing on stamina. I chose the back woods because it's hilly, so keep that in mind. Don't let your horses burn out early since the we'll cover over fifteen jumps and several miles."

I wanted to go *now*. I was so ready for this! Charm would almost rather do cross-country than eat, which was saying something.

Mr. Conner handed us our black vests and we buckled them on. I tightened the chin strap on my helmet and was ready to go.

"Follow me," Mr. Conner said. He tapped his heels against Lexington's sides and the gelding broke into a smooth trot.

Heather and I followed on Aristocrat and Charm. The horses snorted and stretched as they trotted over the grass. I could feel Charm's excitement over not going to the arena. His ears pricked forward and he tugged on the reins, asking for more.

A few strides ahead of us, Mr. Conner let Lexington into a canter. Heather and I shot smiles at each other, then let out our horses. Charm and Aristocrat charged after Lexington and the horses drew even with each other.

I was beside Mr. Conner and Heather was on my right. Charm's mane whipped back and the sunlight glinted off his shoulders. Mr. Conner drew ahead and Heather and I held our horses back so we could follow him. We cantered away from the stable and started up a gentle hill that led to the woods. I leaned forward so I'd keep my balance as Charm started up the climb. He shifted his weight and used his hindquarters to move us up the hill.

When we reached level ground, Mr. Conner slowed Lexington a fraction to line up with Heather and me. "Let them into a *slow* gallop," he said. "We'll gallop until a few yards before the woods, then pull them up to a canter. From there, we'll take the obstacles that cross our path. I've already ridden this way a few times to test it, so it's safe."

Wind whooshed in my ears and when Mr. Conner nodded, we all let our horses out a notch. Charm raced forward, wanting to be in front of Aristocrat. But the darker chestnut wasn't about to let Charm get away with it—he tugged on the reins and quickened his pace. Heather and I were ahead of Mr. Conner and Lexington in seconds and we glanced at each other. If we let the horses go faster, he'd make us go back to the arena.

I sat deeper in the saddle and pulled lightly on the reins, asking Charm to slow. Charm's muzzle dropped back by Aristocrat's shoulder and he shook his head. I thought Heather wasn't going to slow Aristocrat, but she pulled him to a hand gallop and our horses drew even.

Their hooves thundered over the grass. There wasn't anything I'd rather be doing. Charm, happy now that he was even with Aristocrat, settled into a smooth gallop. Mr. Conner galloped Lexington between Charm and Aristocrat, preventing Charm from having such direct eye contact with his nemesis.

We galloped for several yards and Charm's breathing seemed to match my own. Everything—Homecoming, Jacob, Callie, Eric, Paige—seemed to fall away and all I felt was a sense of security and comfort. It felt good to let Charm go and to be away from campus. The three horses' hooves pounded over the ground and all too soon, the woods loomed in front of us.

"Pull them to a canter," Mr. Conner called. "And follow me single file, please."

Heather and I slowed the horses and she let me move Charm behind Lexington. It was a nice gesture—Charm wouldn't be fighting to keep up with Aristocrat, but it also meant Heather was watching me ride. I fought back my nerves. So what if she was? Cross-country was my forte and Heather saw me ride every day in lessons. I wasn't going to mess up.

The horses cantered slowly into the woods and reached a dirt path. Sunlight filtered through the trees and cast shadows on the trail. The path was straight for yards and we started up another hill. We swept past trees that lined the path and Mr. Conner eased Lexington into a trot as we reached a gentle curve. I followed him and when the path straightened, we were trotting next to the creek. Sunlight caught on the multicolored pebbles and I made myself look away, but it was too late. I remembered how just before YENT testing, Charm had developed a fear of going through the creek. Callie had helped me get him over his fear. I blinked furiously, trying to erase the memory from my brain.

Ahead of me, Mr. Conner gathered Lexington and they jumped a fallen tree no more than a foot and a half high.

A few strides later, Charm and I reached the tree. I eased my hands up along his neck and he jumped the tree without pause. A few seconds later, I heard Aristocrat land behind us and we kept trotting down the path as it twisted through the woods.

Mr. Conner turned toward the creek and I leaned back as Charm started down the creek bank. Lexington reached the creek bed and splashed through the knee high water. Water darkened his coat and he looked like steel as he trotted up the bank.

Charm didn't even blink at the creek—he went right in. The coolish water probably felt refreshing to him after cantering and galloping. His shoes clinked against the pebbles and he charged up the bank after Lexington.

When we reached level ground, I pulled Charm to a halt and waited for Heather and Aristocrat to clear the creek bed.

"Go ahead," I said, waving my hand in front of her.

She nodded and let Aristocrat trot by Charm and me. We followed her; Charm's earlier need to overtake Aristocrat had been calmed by this point in the workout.

Mr. Conner let Lexington into a canter and Heather and I followed him. The path straightened and one by one we jumped a stack of hay bales that had been placed across the path. A few strides later, we cleared a log and then I saw the next jump: I almost bounced up and down in the saddle. It was a zigzag—a jump I'd only done a couple of times. The wooden jump had logs that formed a zigzag pattern and the odd shape could cause a refusal if the horse didn't trust the rider. The logs were surrounded by a wooden box and the box was filled with wood chips. The jump wasn't high—it didn't have to be, because the pattern was what often threw off the horses.

I wondered if this was how the rest of the course was designed. Maybe Mr. Conner had set us up with a completely new course that we'd get to use more.

Charm's ears flicked back for a second as we reached the zigzag. Yards in front of us, Mr. Conner moved Lexington, who started to sidestep, back in front of the jump. The gelding shuddered for a second, but took the obstacle. Charm, who'd been watching Lexington, tensed beneath me and I pushed him forward with my hands and legs. I wasn't going to let him stop.

"You got it," I whispered. "C'mon."

Charm's back relaxed and his stride became confident. In front of us, Aristocrat leaped the jump easily and that seemed to give Charm incentive. He approached the zigzag and I kept both legs steady against his sides so he

knew running out wasn't an option. He lifted into the air and tucked his forelegs under his body as we cleared the low jump.

We cantered for several minutes down the trail, weaving around trees until we reached an open clearing. Mr. Conner let Lexington into a faster canter and Heather and I copied him. The field of green looked as if it stretched on forever.

Charm showed no signs of slowing down as we moved over the ground. He hadn't started to sweat yet, but my T-shirt was sticking to my back. We'd lost the shade of the woods when we'd hit the clearing.

We cantered up another hill and the ground leveled. Lexington and then Aristocrat took a brush fence. Charm hopped it easily. A few strides later, we approached an old wooden park bench. All three horses jumped it without pause and we cantered toward the next jump.

I *loved* this! Not only did Heather and I get to observe Mr. Conner ride, but we also got to jump a new course. I loved arena lessons, but sometimes things got stale. And coming out here to a new place where Charm wasn't familiar with his surroundings was good for him.

Mr. Conner started to turn in a half-circle and we were facing the campus, even if we couldn't see it. He eased

Lexington to a trot and we went down a sharper hill. At the bottom of the hill we trotted for two strides before leaping two tiny brush jumps in a row. I watched Heather and Aristocrat for a few seconds, marveling at Heather's form over each jump. She never wavered, and her confidence transmitted to Aristocrat.

"Last jump," Mr. Conner called back to us.

I was sorry the course was over so soon. I knew Charm would take it again if I let him.

Mr. Conner let Lexington canter a bit faster to gain enough momentum to make it over a wooden gate with a small shrub on each side. Lexington, still greener than Charm or Aristocrat, started to rush the fence. Even though Heather was well behind Mr. Conner and Lexington, she slowed Aristocrat a notch in case the gray refused the fence. But Mr. Conner knew how to handle Lexington. He did a half halt and Lexington kept going at the same pace for a few seconds before listening to Mr. Conner. He slowed, collected himself, and lifted into the air. He cleared the gate without even coming close to touching it.

Aristocrat and Heather went next and, as expected, had no problem. I gave Charm rein to let him canter fast. He hadn't lost a bit of energy since we'd started the course.

I counted down the strides in my head and at the right second, Charm leaped into the air. He hit the grass softly on the other side and we joined Heather and Mr. Conner at a trot.

"That was excellent, girls," Mr. Conner said. "Both of you are strong in cross-country and you didn't let any of the new obstacles or the new path become an excuse for allowing your horse to refuse a fence or get nervous."

"Thanks," Heather and I said.

"Let's keep them at a trot to cool down on our way back to the stable," Mr. Conner said. "And be sure to check their legs for heat or any sign of stress after that ride."

We trotted the horses side by side back to the stable. I was pumped after that round. But with every step closer to the stable, I wanted more and more to go back to the woods until Homecoming was over.

When we got back to the stable, I dismounted and loosened Charm's girth. He was going to need extra walking and I wanted to give him a bath. It had been a while since the last time when—*no*. Did not want to think about that. But I couldn't stop the memory. The last time I'd bathed Charm, Eric had helped me because Jasmine had turned

out Charm in the back pasture after it had rained. It had been minutes before my lesson and I'd found Charm coated from ears to tail in mud. Eric had helped me wash him in the outdoor wash stall and we'd ended up turning the hose on each other.

I couldn't help but smile when I remembered the look on Eric's face when I'd swiped mud across his cheek. He'd retaliated and by the end, Charm was the cleanest of all of us. I sighed. Did not want to think about Eric. It didn't do any good. There was no chance of getting him back and I had to let him move on. I'd done enough damage.

I removed Charm's tack and he waited for me just outside the door while I hung up his bridle and put away his saddle. I grabbed a bucket, container of horse shampoo, coat conditioner and a sponge. I untied Charm's cotton lead line from the tie ring and we started walking outside. We passed Black Jack's stall and I slowed. The stall door was opening and Callie led him out into the aisle. I looked at her face and knew immediately that something was up. I was her former BFF—I could tell when there was something going on. Her lips were pressed together and she stared at the ground. I couldn't walk away without saying *something*.

"Callie?" I asked, my voice barely above a whisper. "Everything okay?"

Callie's expression changed from worry to anger. She shook her head. "Are you kidding me? You're the *last* person I want to talk to. Don't say a word to me again. Ever."

My throat tightened and I led Charm down the aisle and outside. I hated this. Every second of it. But I'd done what I'd had to do to protect Callie. And I couldn't go back on that now.

11

PAIGE = HOMECOMING OBSESSED

ON MY WAY BACK TO MY ROOM, I STOPPED by the girl's bathroom to shower and change. Paige was out, so I decided to text her to see if she wanted to meet up and study in the common room together.

When u get back wanna study in com room? I sent the text and started gathering my books. I had enough to do that I could go and get a head start.

My phone beeped a couple of minutes later.

Just finished w HC committee—b there in 5

I deleted the message. At least if we had to work, Paige wouldn't have any time to talk about Homecoming.

In the common room I spread my stuff on the round table. If I sat on the couch I'd get too comfy and would probably fall asleep. I took the egg that Jacob and I shared for health class and set it on the table, then snapped a picture of it. I was definitely going to get an A in this class—no doubt. I'd wanted to give the egg to Jacob yesterday when I'd seen him in the hallway, but things had been too weird with Callie.

I pulled out my history book and started reading the assigned chapter. Mr. Spellman's class wasn't too hard, but he always assigned a lot of required reading. I'd read a few pages when I heard flip-flops approach the common room.

Paige walked inside, her arms full of green folders.

"What are those?" I asked.

She grinned at me. "Details for the dance!"

Did *every* sentence about Homecoming have to end in an exclamation point?

"Oh, cool," I said. "I'm sure it'll be great."

Paige put the folders on the table and flipped open one. "It's going to be *amazing*. Seriously. I'd tell you every detail, but I don't want to ruin the surprise for you."

"Yeah," I said. "You definitely don't want to do that. I love surprises."

And if I hear one more thing about it, I'll go insane, I thought, but smiled at Paige.

"Are you the first person in Canterwood history who

doesn't have homework?" I asked, nodding at the folders. "Because then I'd be so jealous."

Paige sighed. "I have homework, but I really want to go over all of this first."

I nodded, not saying anything, and went back to my textbook. I wanted to talk to Paige about *so* many things, like my party and what we were going to do over fall break, but all she wanted to talk about was Homecoming.

"So, has anyone heard from Jasmine?" Paige asked.

I looked up slowly. "That's kind of random. Why would any of us hear from her?"

Paige shrugged. "I don't know. I guess I didn't expect her to contact any of you, but I kind of wonder where she is and stuff."

"I don't care as long as it's not here." I uncapped my pen pointedly, trying to signal to Paige that I was done talking about Jasmine.

"How are Julia and Alison doing?" Paige asked. "They have to be feeling awesome now that the truth about what really happened is finally out."

I stiffened in my seat. I knew Paige well enough to know where she was going with this. If I let her, she'd make the conversation about my party. She was using Julia and Alison's situation as a way to ease into talking about

my party. I wanted to talk to her about it, but not like this. Not when she'd spent so much time talking about poor Jasmine and Homecoming.

"Julia and Alison are happy. Glad to be back on the team." I pointed to my book. "I've really got to get this done, okay?"

Paige shrank back a little. "Yeah. Sorry. I'll go get my homework."

She gathered her folders and left the common room. I folded my arms on the table and laid my head on the desk. This was *ridiculous*. I couldn't even have a normal conversation with my roommate anymore! She was obsessed with Homecoming *and* with trying to find a way to prove that I'd lied about what had happened with Jacob at my party. And I was getting tired of it—I wanted to tell her the truth on my own terms.

Paige entered the common room without a word moments later and we both got to work. Neither of us talked as we did our homework and the tension in the room was crazy. I was considering saying I was done with my homework, even though I wasn't, and telling Paige I had to run to the stable to pick up something I'd forgotten. Just as I started to close my book, my phone buzzed.

4got 2 get egg from u yest. Wanna trade now?

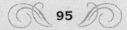

It took me two point five seconds to type a response. *Sure. Meet me outside Winchester.*

I picked up the egg, its padded box that Jacob had made, and our notebook, leaving my books spread open on the table.

"Back in a sec," I said. "I've got pass my egg to Jacob."

"'Kay," was all Paige said.

I left the room and felt immediate relief the second I got out. I hurried down the hallway and when I pushed open the door, Jacob was leaning casually against the railing. I tried not to smile when I saw him, but I couldn't stop myself.

"Hi," I said. My voice sounded shy and it felt like it was the first time we'd met.

"Hey," Jacob said, his voice soft. Our eyes met and, for a second, all I could think about was how much I'd missed the tingly feeling I'd had whenever I'd looked into his eyes.

Stop it, I said to myself. *He's with Callie. Just like you wanted. You had your chance to be with him.*

I thrust the egg and notebook in his direction, then took a step back toward the door.

"I logged everything in the notebook," I said. "If you just write that you took it tonight, we'll be ready when we turn it in tomorrow."

"Great." Jacob looked at the egg, then back up at me. "I know we'll get a good grade. There's no way we won't."

"Yeah, we really did carry that thing everywhere," I said.

As I spoke, I tried to think of something—anything—to talk about to keep him here. But I knew better. I didn't need to be talking to Jacob. I should have been inside, doing homework and not chatting with my ex–best friend's boyfriend. I didn't need anyone to see us together and think there was something going on.

He had a look on his face as if he wanted to tell me something. I could feel it. But if this had anything to do with Callie, I definitely didn't want to know. *But maybe it has nothing to do with her,* I thought. It could be about a zillion things—school, parents, whatever.

Paige was waiting for me in the common room, probably counting the minutes of how long I'd been out here with Jacob.

"I've got to get back inside," I said, tipping my head back in the direction of the door.

"Oh." Jacob put his free hand in his pocket. "Okay."

"Bye." I turned, pulled open the door and left him standing on the steps before he could say another word.

12

EGG FREE
AT LAST

I WALKED INTO MR. SPELLMAN'S HISTORY
class on Wednesday afternoon dreading the period. It was
my least favorite class because I shared it with Eric *and*
Jacob. They hadn't interacted during class since my party,
but they were about to be forced to. Soon.

"Class," Mr. Spellman said. "I wanted to remind you
all that after fall break, your group projects will begin."

I looked at Jacob, then at Eric. They were both in the
same group. Luckily, I wasn't with them. If Mr. Spellman
had assigned me to their project, I would have asked for
a transfer. At least they wouldn't have to start working
together until after fall break. Maybe a week away would
do everyone some good. We all needed some space from
each other.

"Today, I want you all to get into your assigned groups and begin discussing about how you're going to handle your project. Go ahead and gather your group members."

I watched, frozen, as Eric and Jacob glanced at each other from their seats. Eric got up first and moved to join the other people in their group who had gotten together by one girl's desk.

Jacob stood and walked over, keeping two people between him and Eric. I almost couldn't breathe, watching them being forced to interact with each other and stand so close together. They *hated* each other and now they'd have to spend time on a group project. The odds of them being paired up together had been ridiculous. I'd almost fallen out of my seat when Mr. Spellman had announced the groups.

I looked up, surprised when I realized my group had huddled around my desk. I guess because I hadn't moved, they'd all come to join me. The three people I didn't know—two guys and a girl—scooted their desks closer to mine.

"Introductions first I guess?" asked a guy with black hair.

"Yeah, let's," said the girl. "I'm Diana."

"Sasha," I said.

"Van."

"And I'm Oliver," said the other guy.

Diana got out a notebook and wrote *History Project* across the top of the page. "Want to just toss around a bunch of ideas and see what we come up with?" she asked.

"That sounds good," I said. I sat back in my chair and let them talk. I nodded along and pretended to listen as they talked about ideas for our project. I should have been offering suggestions, but I kept stealing glances over at Eric and Jacob. Their group was sitting at the far corner of the room and they weren't even looking at each other.

"So, if we all brainstorm over break," said Diana. "Then we'll have way more ideas when we meet when classes start again."

"Sounds good," I heard myself say. This was one time when I was cool with sitting back and letting other people take control. Normally, I'd want to be in charge and let my type A personality take over. But I didn't care that much. I just couldn't stop watching Jacob and Eric.

When it was time for health class, I felt like I'd downed too many energy drinks. Witnessing the tension between Jacob and Eric had made me nervous during history, and

I hadn't been able to shake the feeling all day that something was up with Jacob. The more I watched him, the more I was convinced that something was wrong. He was fidgety and he seemed on edge every time I saw him.

I sat down in health class and looked away when Jacob walked into the room. I couldn't keep looking at him for signs of whatever I imagined was going on—I was making myself crazy.

Paige walked into the classroom and took her seat. We smiled at each other. Ever since the awkwardness in the common room last night, we'd both gone out of our way to be friendlier to each other. I didn't want to fight with Paige about something as stupid as Homecoming. I wanted to go into fall break with things good between us.

"Hi, class," Ms. Utz said, walking into the room. "As you're all aware, today you'll turn in your reports and will relinquish custody of your egg. Unless, of course, you want to keep it."

No one wanted that. We were all ready to hand over our egg, and be finished with this project. I'd hated it the second we'd been given the assignment, but Jacob had at least tried to make it fun by drawing a face on the egg. He'd been a great partner and he'd made it easy on me for us to work together.

Ms. Utz moved to the center of the front of the classroom and looked at us. "I've got a few questions for you all. Krista and Josh, what did you learn from this project?"

Krista looked down at her egg and then up at Ms. Utz. "Well, I learned that it was harder than I thought not to break the egg."

Josh grinned. "We only broke it twice."

That made Krista blush. "*Only* twice?"

The class laughed and so did Ms. Utz.

"So you realized that you needed to be more careful than you thought," Ms. Utz said. "It may have taken you two tries, but at least you *did* figure it out."

Krista and Josh nodded. Ms. Utz collected their journal and egg.

"Let's hear from . . ." Ms. Utz's eyes scanned the room. "Sasha and Jacob. What about you? What did this experience teach you?"

Jacob glanced over at me and I nodded, letting him go first.

"It was more difficult to coordinate schedules than I thought it would be," Jacob said. "Finding times we both could meet wasn't easy."

"It was also hard to take the egg everywhere," I said.

"I always worried it would get broken or that I'd leave it somewhere."

"I kept forgetting about it," Jacob said. "I almost left it behind a zillion times. Now that the project's over, I've finally gotten used to carrying it around."

Ms. Utz smiled. "That figures, right? But you and Sasha made it work, you never broke your egg, and you did eventually learn to remember to take it with you."

Jacob glanced at me and there was a weird look on his face. It disappeared when Utz collected the journal and egg from him. *Ignore it,* I told myself. It wasn't up to me to figure out what was going on with Jacob. And maybe I was just seeing things that weren't there. But even as I thought it, I knew I was lying to myself. Something was *definitely* up.

13

OVER

EVEN THE STABLE HAD BEEN ATTACKED BY Homecoming. Riders had put up signs and streamers— all out of reach of curious horses. Even the bathroom and the hallway to Mr. Conner's office had been assaulted with green and gold. I couldn't believe he'd let people decorate his stable. I hurried to grab Charm's tack so I could get to his stall and escape.

"Charm," I said, wrapping my arms around his neck. I hugged him as if I hadn't seen him for weeks, even though it had only been since yesterday. "Ugh, boy," I said. "Everything's a mess!"

Charm took a sip from his water bucket and I clipped the lead line onto his halter. I led him into the aisle and walked him all the way to the back of the stable until we found an empty pair of crossties. I needed to be away from everyone for a few minutes.

"As if it wasn't enough that the entire campus is decorated for Homecoming, the stable was taken over too," I said to him.

I took a dandy brush out of Charm's tack box and started brushing dirt off his legs. Mike or Doug must have turned him out this morning because he had a grass stain on his sock.

"You're all set for Homecoming," I grumbled. I walked over to the wash stall beside him and filled a bucket with warm, soapy water. I crouched down and scrubbed until the grass stain was gone. Charm was quiet as I started his normal grooming routine. I had time, so I put extra effort into brushing every speck of dirt from his coat and combing his mane and tail until they were tangle free. After Charm's hooves were clean, I picked up his white saddle pad and placed it on his back, then lowered the saddle on top of it. Charm didn't move while I tightened the girth and ran down the stirrups. I released him from the crossties and bridled him. With my helmet in hand I started toward the arena.

At least Heather was the only one in my class. I almost shook my head at the irony of that. Weeks ago, I would

have done anything to avoid going to class with just Heather. But everything had changed during Homecoming week. She was the only person I could talk to who wasn't obsessed with it. *Aside from Jacob,* I thought. I wondered what he was doing. Maybe he was at track practice. Or doing homework. He could be at the media center with his friends playing video games.

Stop it, I said to myself. I had no reason to be thinking about Jacob.

I kept my gaze straight ahead as we walked down the aisle, avoiding looking at the decorations. I led Charm through the wide entrance into the indoor arena and put on my helmet. I looked up and down the arena, but it was empty. Weird—Heather was almost always here before me.

I gathered the reins in my left hand and stuck my toe in the stirrup. With a light bounce I pushed myself up from the ground and swung my other leg over Charm's hindquarters. I settled myself in the saddle, then nudged my heels against Charm's sides. He moved into an easy walk and after a couple of minutes, I let him into a trot. I posted, catching a glimpse of myself in the mirror. My heels were down, my back was straight without look-ing stiff, and my hands were balanced just right over Charm's neck.

I looked up when Heather jogged into the arena with Aristocrat beside her. She halted him and mounted.

"Where were you?" I asked. "You were almost late."

Heather shook her head. "You won't believe it."

"What?"

"Julia, Alison, and I saw—" Heather started, but Mr. Conner walked into the arena. Heather closed her mouth.

"Saw what?" I whispered. "Tell me!"

But Heather shook her head. "After," she mouthed.

I groaned to myself. Whatever she'd seen had been good. And now I had to concentrate through an entire lesson and wait for it to be over before she'd be able to tell me.

Mr. Conner smiled at us as he walked into the center of the arena. His tall black boots shone in the sunlight that streamed through the arena windows. He was wearing breeches and I wondered if he'd just finished working with Lexington.

"Hi, girls," he said. "If you're warmed up and ready to go, let's work on jumping today."

At least that would help keep my mind off whatever Heather had to tell me.

"I want you to dismount and swap horses," Mr. Conner said.

I swung my leg over the back of the saddle and kicked my foot out of the stirrup. I hopped to the ground and handed the Charm's reins to Heather. She gave me Aristocrat's and I gathered the reins in my hand and mounted. The chestnut gelding flicked his ears back and forth, probably anxious at having someone new on his back.

I patted his neck. "It's okay, boy," I said. "You know me."

I watched Heather mount Charm and he was quiet under her. He glanced at Aristocrat and saw me on his back, but he stayed still and listened to Heather. Mr. Conner had made us swap horses during lessons before and, at first, I'd hated riding any other horse. But now I was beginning to understand Mr. Conner's point that riding different horses was great training. I learned something new from every horse I rode. I had a feeling Heather liked riding Charm even though she'd never admit it.

"Take them around at a trot, then a canter," Mr. Conner said. "Just a couple of laps to acquaint yourself with your different horse. Then we'll take a few jumps."

I squeezed my legs against Aristocrat's sides and angled him toward the wall. His trot was so smooth that I didn't even need to post. In front of us, Heather and

Charm moved well together and I felt proud that Charm was listening to Heather. I wondered if he could sense that Heather and I weren't total enemies anymore.

After a lap, I let Aristocrat canter and I smiled at how fast he responded to my cues. He was attentive, but not overly sensitive.

"All right," Mr. Conner said. "Pull them up and let's discuss the course."

Heather and I slowed the horses and brought them to a stop in front of him.

"You're going to take four verticals and a triple combination," Mr. Conner said.

I shivered a little at the mention of *triple* on a strange horse.

"The verticals increase in height and you'll need to be prepared for the triple," Mr. Conner said. "Remember that you don't know the horse you're riding as well as you do your own, so be mindful of that."

Heather and I nodded. I was ready to jump no matter what horse I rode.

"Heather," Mr. Conner said, motioning to her. "You'll ride first. Sasha, while Heather rides, I want you to watch Charm. It'll give you a new perspective on his movements to see someone else riding him."

"Okay," I said.

Heather squeezed her legs against Charm's sides and encouraged him into a trot. He looked smooth and together as he moved away from Aristocrat and me. Heather let Charm into a canter and I watched as he tossed his head once when he changed gaits. He was excited about jumping, but Heather didn't let him get away with it. She took him away from the jumps and made him circle again to let him know he had to be calm before they started.

When Charm completed the circle, Heather turned him toward the course and this time, Charm kept his head down and didn't rush.

Charm's canter was collected as he moved toward the first vertical. He pushed off with his haunches and leaped into the air over the yellow and white striped poles. He landed almost without a sound and Heather was already looking ahead to the next jump.

Charm's stride was rhythmic as he cantered to the next vertical and cleared the blue poles that were a couple of inches higher than the first jump.

He pointed his ears forward and I realized he was getting overconfident. His attention span was waning and Heather realized it as it was happening. She did a half halt, closing her fingers around the reins, and Charm listened to her. He tilted an ear back at her, paying attention again, and they popped over the third vertical. One more to go and then it was the triple. Sometimes Charm and I had timing issues, and I realized I needed to do more of what Heather had done—be prepared for Charm to rush and keep his attention on *me*—not the jumps.

Heather rose out of the saddle before the final vertical and Charm snapped his forelegs perfectly under his body, tucking them under. He landed with his back hooves inches away from the jump and they started making a turn around the side of the arena to approach the triple combo.

Heather's eyes never left the space between Charm's ears. She sank her weight into her heels, easing him just before the first jump. Charm was ready. He flew over the first obstacle, took two strides and then left the ground again for the second. Heather kept his pace even and didn't give him a chance to get distracted. Charm jumped the final part of the triple and a smiling Heather rode him back over to us.

"That was great, Heather," Mr. Conner said. "Charm does have a tendency to become excited on course and you kept him focused. The half halt is a great tool when a horse starts to stop paying attention." He turned to me.

"Sasha, I've seen you use that before with Charm and I'd like to see you implement it more when necessary."

"I will," I said. And he was right. A while ago I would have been embarrassed that Heather had done something with Charm that I hadn't been doing as well. But now I didn't feel like I wanted to knock her off my horse.

"Good," Mr. Conner said. "Whenever you're ready, Sasha, go ahead and take the course with Aristocrat."

My fingers were a little slippery on the reins. I didn't want to mess up—especially not on Heather's horse. But Aristocrat was a total pro and I was sure he'd listen to me, even if he'd much rather have Heather riding him.

I didn't want to spend too much time circling him and making myself nervous, so I closed my legs around his sides and urged him into a trot. After a few strides, I gave him more rein and the chestnut flowed into a canter without hesitation.

I pointed him at the first vertical and didn't have time to think before he flew into the air and soared over the fence. It was almost as if I was along for the ride and he didn't need me to do anything. He gathered himself and I rose into the two-point position just before taking off over the second vertical. Aristocrat jumped with ease, landed, and moved with confidence to the next jump.

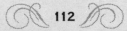

Despite the fact that he and Charm didn't get along, I couldn't help but appreciate him. His movements were gorgeous and he was easy to handle. Even though he was a top-notch Thoroughbred, an inexperienced rider would probably be safe on him.

We finished the verticals and I sucked in a breath just before the first jump of the triple. Timing was everything. If we messed up one part, we could knock the rest of the rails. Aristocrat jumped the first vertical with room to spare, shortened his stride and two seconds later we were in the air and clearing the middle jump. We landed and he didn't need me to do anything—he left the ground at the right second and we jumped the final part of the combo. We circled back to Heather and Mr. Conner.

"Nice job, boy," I said.

Mr. Conner smiled at me. "Good ride, Sasha. Aristocrat is an experienced jumper, but that's sometimes a curse for his rider."

I tilted my head. "What do you mean?"

Mr. Conner's eyes focused on me. "Did you pay as much attention while riding Aristocrat as you would have on Charm? Did you relax because you knew Aristocrat had more experience?"

Ugh. I didn't know it had been obvious!

"A little," I said. "But Aristocrat didn't need as much guidance. He knew what he was doing and I didn't feel like I had to give him as much direction."

"But you also cannot go on autopilot," Mr. Conner said. "Every horse needs instruction from his rider. You cannot let the horse make the decisions about when to jump and how fast or slow to go even if you think the horse is capable of deciding."

I nodded, realizing I'd made a huge mistake. "You're right," I said. "I shouldn't have let his experience level factor into how much attention I paid to him."

"Good," Mr. Conner said. "You'll be ready the next time you ride another horse. Great lesson, both of you, and see you next class."

Heather and I dismounted and swapped reins.

"So tell me now," I said. "What did you hear?"

Heather shook her head. "Can we at least cool the horses? And I'm not telling you here where anyone could overhear it. Just chill. Meet Julia, Alison, and me in the hayloft in half an hour."

"Are you kidding me?! You're going to make me wait even longer?" I wanted to shake the secret out of Heather.

Heather rolled her eyes. "Silver, with your ridiculous record about not knowing what's going on around campus, you probably wouldn't hear about this for a week if it wasn't for me."

And she led Aristocrat out of the arena and away from me before I could say another word.

Heather never got any less infuriating. Ever.

I hurried through cooling, untacking, and grooming Charm. I checked the time on my phone. Still five more minutes before I could meet them. As much as I wanted to hear what Heather had to say, I'd already made myself look desperate for news. So I wasn't showing up until exactly thirty minutes after she told me to meet her.

Thirty-*one* minutes later, I climbed the ladder and stepped onto the platform of the hayloft. No one but Mike, Doug, and Mr. Conner were supposed to come up here, but I'd seen Mike and Doug trimming the grass in an empty pasture and Mr. Conner was teaching a lesson.

"You're late," Julia snapped, peering at me from behind a stack of hay bales. "Get back here, already."

I didn't argue, I just followed her. Alison and Heather were waiting, each seated on a hay bale. I took an empty bale next to Alison and she was practically bouncing.

"Ohhhhmiiiigod," Alison said. "You'll *never* ever guess what we heard just before your lesson."

I looked around at them and suddenly felt a little

nervous. Whatever it was, I didn't want it to have anything to do with me. Or Homecoming.

"Heather's been taunting me with it for forever,"
I said. "So just tell me."

Heather leaned closer and I knew it was something big.
They hadn't called me up here for nothing.

"We were walking down the side aisle to the tack room
to chat before we got our stuff," Heather said. "We heard
people talking inside and when we stopped to listen, we
realized it was Callie and Jacob."

I grasped a fistful of hay. Part of me didn't want to ask,
but I couldn't help it. "What was going on?"

"Jacob apologized to Callie for being so busy lately,"
Alison said. "He said he'd been unfair to her and he was
sorry."

Whew. I let go of the hay.

"He said his parents are making him crazy about his
grades and he's juggling a lot with track and everything
else going on with school," Julia added. She picked at a
piece of hay.

"I'm glad he explained to her what was going on,"
I said. "I'd seen them together and he was being weird. At
least Callie knows what's up and she won't be worried."

"Sasha," Heather interjected. She paused and shifted,

crossing one leg over the other. "Callie won't be worried anymore because . . . Jacob broke up with her."

I stared at her. It was all I could do. It was like I forgot how to speak or move.

"What?" I finally said. "He did *what?"*

"Shhh," Heather said. "Don't be so loud. He told her the timing was wrong and he was sorry, but they couldn't be together."

It was almost too much. My brain couldn't process what Heather was saying.

"What did she say?" I managed to ask.

"Callie was crying," Alison said, her voice soft. "She wanted to work things out so they could stay together, but Jacob insisted they had to break up."

I looked at Heather and her eyes met mine.

"Callie and Jacob are over," she said.

14

HIDE OUT

FOR THE REST OF THE AFTERNOON I HID IN the library. On the top floor. In one of the locked study rooms. Without telling anyone where I was.

Every five seconds my emotions changed. At first all I could think about was looking for Callie and comforting her. Jacob was her first boyfriend and she had to be a wreck. I knew she was in pain and it killed me not to be able to be there for her as she went through her first breakup.

After I thought about Callie, my mind went to Jacob. His claims about school, parents, and sports were probably all true, but it wasn't the reason he'd broken up with Callie. I knew it. And it made me feel so guilty. But when that melted away, just for a second, I wondered what

would happen if we *ever* tried again. I knew we couldn't—
not after everything we'd gone through to protect Callie
from the truth the night of my party.

I sat in the library until just before dusk. My phone
buzzed and I opened it to see a text from Paige.

Where r u? need 2 get ready 4 bonfire!

Oh, my God. I rubbed my eyes. I'd completely forgotten about that. Callie, Jacob, Eric, and I along with the
other nominees were all forced to go to the bonfire since
we were junior royal court nominees. Headmistress Drake
would be there so there was *no* way I could back out.

B rite there, I texted Paige.

I left the library and walked back to Winchester. I had
to tell Paige what was going on before we got to the bonfire. I had no clue how she'd react to the news. I knew
she'd be upset for Callie, but I wondered if that would
raise more questions from her about what really happened
between Jacob and me at my party.

I opened the door to our room, barely realizing that
I'd even walked down the Winchester hallway, and stepped
inside. Paige turned around from her spot in front of our
mirror and looked at me.

"What's wrong?" she asked. "Something happened—I
can see it in your face."

I sat at the edge of my bed and pulled off my riding boots.

Paige sat on her desk chair and swiveled it to look at me. "You can tell me—whatever it is."

"I know," I said. "It's just hard to talk about." I paused, taking a breath. "I was at the stable and just before my lesson, Heather told me she needed to tell me something."

"Uh-oh."

"I know. I had to go through the entire lesson just waiting for her to tell me and I thought I was going to die. Then when it was finally over and I asked her, she told me to meet her at the hayloft with Julia and Alison in half an hour."

Paige shook her head. "So typical Heather. Dangling something in front of you and then saying wait. Again."

"Agreed. So after half an hour I met them. They said they'd overheard Callie and Jacob in the tack room."

I watched Paige's face, but her expression gave away nothing. She sat still—waiting for me to finish.

"Jacob told Callie that his parents were on him about his grades and he was feeling tons of pressure with sports. He knew he wasn't being a good boyfriend and he apologized to her."

Paige leaned back into her chair. "She must feel better now, right? I mean, if he had all of that going on, she must have sensed that things were off and he was going through something."

I wrung my hands together. "I doubt she feels better. Jacob broke up with her." I whispered the last sentence.

"Oh, no!" Paige's shoulders slumped. "Poor Callie! She must be a mess. Her first boyfriend."

"I know. She's got to be so upset and I really do feel bad for her." I had to choose every word carefully so that Paige didn't think I still cared about Callie and missed her as my BFF. If Paige knew that, it would totally blow my cover story with Jacob.

"The last thing she probably wants to do is come to the bonfire," Paige said.

And it's the last thing I want to do, I wanted to say.

"You're probably right, but she has to," I said.

I pulled a jean skirt, platform wedge sandals, and a V-neck sweater from my closet. I couldn't talk about Callie and Jacob anymore.

"I'll be ready to go in half an hour," I said. "You can wait or go without me, if you want."

"I'll wait," Paige said, shrugging. "You won't be too long and it doesn't start till it gets dark, anyway."

In the bathroom I closed the door and sat on the edge of the bathtub. It was going to be a long night.

15

CAN'T LET THE NIGHT GO UP IN FLAMES

PAIGE AND I WALKED TO THE BACK OF THE campus, near the spot at the woods where I'd ridden the new cross-country course.

"You look nervous," Paige said. "Don't be. It'll be okay. Really. The nominees *have* to be there, but at least you all don't have to do anything together."

"But the odds of us all running into each other are ridiculous," I said. "You know I'll see *someone*."

Paige touched my arm. "Don't worry. Even if you do, just walk away. It doesn't have to turn into a thing."

That made my head jerk back a little. Did Paige think I always turned social events into "things?"

"I don't want it to turn into anything. I just want to be there until I can leave and then go."

Paige pressed her lips together, not saying anything. We walked the final distance across campus where the glow of the bonfire reached into the sky and illuminated darkness. I loved the smell of burning wood. The sparks of the fire flew into the air and shattered into ash.

We reached the fire and it was so much warmer, even though the night air was cooling around us.

"Hey," Ryan said, walking up to us. He grabbed Paige's hand and smiled at her, then me.

"Hi," Paige said. She touched his upper arm with her free hand.

"A bunch of people are roasting marshmallows over there," Ryan said, looking at us. "Want to?"

Paige nodded. "Sure." She looked over at me. "Sash?"

I looked around to the spot Ryan was talking about. Roasting marshmallows sounded like a popular spot.

"You go," I said. "I'm going to go find a hot dog or something."

"You sure?" Paige asked.

"Totally. Go and I'll meet up with you later."

"'Kay," Paige said. "Sounds good."

Hand in hand, Paige and Ryan walked away to the other side of the bonfire. I tried not to feel anxious about being on my own since I'd told them to go, but I couldn't stop running through scenarios. What if I saw Jacob? Or Eric? Or Callie?

I was most worried about seeing Callie. I didn't trust myself not to run up to her, hug her, and tell her that she was going to be okay. Panic was just starting to rise in my chest when I saw Heather, Alison, and Julia walk up to me.

"Is this not the lamest thing ever?" Heather asked. Lame as she claimed it to be, she'd dressed for it, too, in a black skirt, sandals, and V-neck T-shirt.

"So lame," I said. "We're *forced* to be here. How wrong is that?"

Alison rolled her eyes at us, grinning. "Stop it! It's Homecoming week. It only happens once a year, so embrace it. Stop whining and just enjoy it. It's a bonfire. Have fun!"

My eyes met Heather's and we rolled our eyes.

"Yeah, yeah," I grumbled. "Bonfire. Hot dogs. Yay."

Alison grabbed my arm and steered me around to the other side of the fire. "You're going to have fun," she said. "So deal."

I let her pull me over to where teachers had set up a food station. The Trio and I readied our hot dogs. We headed over to an empty spot near the fire and stuck our hot dogs near the flames.

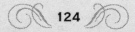

"I'm eating two and saving room for s'mores," Julia said. "Did you see how many bags of marshmallows there are?"

"I was too busy trying not to spear myself with the hot-dog roaster," I said.

We twirled our hot dogs for a few more minutes, watching how the seventh graders had clumped together on one side of the fire and we and the rest of the eighth graders had staked out our own space on the other side.

"So glad we never looked like that," Heather said, nodding her head in the seventh graders' direction. "They look all scared and pathetic."

"*We* never looked like that," Julia said. She glanced at me. "But admit it, Sasha, you totally did."

I couldn't help but smile. "Okay, okay! That's true. At least I'm not like that now."

Heather stared at me as if she was going to argue, but smiled instead. "Yeah, you've gotten a little better."

"Ha-ha," I said. "Thanks a lot."

We finished roasting our hot dogs and took them over to the table with plates and everything we needed to fix our hot dogs. We got plastic cups of soda and handfuls of chips while Alison looked around for a good spot to sit. I grabbed one of the blankets the school had stored in a bin for us to use.

"Over there?" she pointed. Julia, Heather, and I nodded. She'd picked a spot that was quiet and just far enough away from the bonfire that we wouldn't feel like we were melting.

We put down our stuff and spread out the—what else—*green* blanket and started eating. Ketchup from Alison's hot dog oozed out and plopped onto her plate.

"Oops," she said, giggling.

"At least it landed on your plate and not your lap," Julia said. "Remember when you spilled mustard down the front of your shirt just before that big show a couple of years ago?"

Alison tilted her head back, looking up at the black sky. "Omigod, that was so awful. I just *had* to have a hot dog and of course I didn't bring another shirt."

"Did you show with the stain?" I asked.

"Nope," Heather said. She grinned. "In some mysterious, strange way, another girl's shirt disappeared from her clothing bag."

I munched on a barbecue-flavored chip. "You stole someone's shirt? Did you give it back?"

"After Alison's class, we did," Heather said. "So yes, *Jasmine* got her shirt back."

I burst into laughter. "Omigod!"

All of us started laughing. We glanced up when someone walked by the end of our blanket.

Callie. The fire light flickered on her face and I could
see anger in her eyes, even in the semi-darkness.

My laughter stopped instantly.

She glared down at us and shook her head as she
stomped by. The Trio exchanged glances. Without saying
anything, we all went back to our food.

16

JUST TALK TO ME

I STAYED WITH THE TRIO FOR A WHILE longer, then Ben walked over and pulled Julia up off the blanket.

"Want to roast marshmallows with me?" he asked.

"Definitely," she said.

"I need another soda," Alison said, peering into her empty cup.

"Me too," Heather said.

"I think I'm going to go find Paige," I said. "I gave her space with Ryan for a while, but I know she wanted to hang with me, too."

Alison and Heather nodded and got up off the blanket. We split up and I started looking for Paige. There were a lot of people and it was hard to make out faces in the shadows. I walked past clumps of students and someone grabbed my arm.

I turned to find Jacob's handsome face glowing in the firelight.

"I can't talk now," I said. "I'm looking for Paige."

He released my arm. "Sasha, please. Just talk to me for a second."

"No," I said. "People can't keep seeing us talk."

I moved away from Jacob and left him standing there.

"Sasha!" Paige popped into view, a s'more in one hand and a bottle of root beer in the other. "I'm so glad I found you. Ryan just went to get more marshmallows. You have to hang with us for the rest of the night."

I smiled, not wanting her to see I was upset. "Actually, can we talk for a sec? Alone?"

Paige frowned and stared at me. "Of course. Did something happen?"

"We need to walk away from everyone else."

Paige followed me to the edge of the woods and we stood in the semi-darkness, away from the fire and the crowd.

"Just tell me," Paige said. She touched my elbow. "What's going on?"

I couldn't hold it in for another second. "You've been

right this whole time. I've been lying to you about what happened at my party. I'm so, so sorry, Paige."

Paige rubbed her forehead. "Jacob *did* try to kiss you, didn't he?"

"Yes."

"Sasha, I knew you'd never do anything like that. Why didn't you just tell me?" Paige's eyes were full of confusion.

"I don't know! I guess I was afraid to make him look like the bad guy and I *never* wanted Callie to know the truth, even though I know you'd wouldn't tell her."

"No," Paige said, her tone soft. "I'd never do that."

"I should have told you that night, but it just felt like the right thing to do not to tell anyone—Jacob and I both agreed."

Paige was quiet for a minute. "You gave up your other best friend to protect him. You lost so much—I'm sorry."

"I just wish I'd told you sooner. You would have been there for me. I'm really, really sorry I lied to you, Paige."

Paige leaned over, hugging me. "I'm sorry you felt like you had to. But I'm your best friend. You can always tell me anything. I'm glad I finally know the truth. I'd known something was off and—"

Paige stopped talking when footsteps approached and Ryan came into view.

"Hey," he said to us. "Paige, the Homecoming committee is looking for you. They need to know where the extra packages of Hershey's bars are."

I looked at Paige, waiting for her to tell Ryan we were having a chat and she'd help them when she could.

"Okay," Paige said. She smiled at him and squeezed my hand. "I've got to go. But thanks for talking to me. We can talk as soon as I finish with the committee."

And she and Ryan left me standing there.

This was ridiculous. I hurried away from the fire and walked across the grass and to the sidewalk, my shoes thudding on the pavement. Obviously, Homecoming came before best friends.

I took a breath and I saw Jacob's face in the firelight. I sighed, wishing I could think of anything else. But now my mind was stuck on him.

He was single.

I was on my own.

But it didn't matter. We had to stay apart.

17

"SPIRIT" DAY?
DON'T THINK SO.

WHEN PAIGE AND I WOKE UP, WE WERE BOTH quiet. It was Spirit Day, but it definitely didn't feel like that in our dorm. We didn't say much as we got dressed. I pulled on a hunter green skirt over black leggings and a gold T-shirt. Paige dressed in dark green cords and a white T-shirt with gold stitching.

Neither of us said a word as we brushed our teeth, flatironed our hair, and put on makeup. It was the most awkward morning we'd *ever* had.

I grabbed my bookbag, slinging it over my shoulder, and picked up the rest of my books off my bed.

"Sasha," Paige said.

I turned to glance at her, really looking at her for the

first time since the bonfire. I noticed the dark circles under her eyes and her pale face.

"What?" I asked.

Paige looked down, then back up at me. "I'm so sorry about last night. I should have talked to you for at least a few more minutes instead of rushing off to work on Homecoming."

I nodded, not responding. I'd pretended to be asleep last night when Paige had gotten back—I hadn't been ready to talk. But I didn't want to walk out now without saying anything. Paige really was sorry and I knew she hadn't meant to hurt my feelings.

"It's okay," I said. "Everyone's stressed out right now and there are a million things going on." I paused for a second. "I know I've been totally anti-Homecoming and I haven't been fair since it's something that's important to you."

Paige looked at me, twisting a lock of her red-gold hair.

"I know how much you love Homecoming and I want to be better about being excited for you, even if I'm not," I said.

"Thanks," Paige said. "And I know there are lots of things going on for you related to Homecoming. You've got Callie, Jacob, and Eric all there. I haven't been as sensitive to that as I should have been."

"You were just excited about Homecoming," I said. "I was never upset about that. It was just hard for me to think about going to Homecoming when Callie, Jacob, and everyone else were going to be there. But you know I was excited for you, too. It's a big deal that you and Ryan got nominated and I hope I didn't make that any less special for you."

Paige shook her head. "Please. Stop it. You totally didn't. There are two days left of Homecoming and I want us to just have fun the rest of the time. *And* I want you to be comfortable doing whatever you want. I know you have to do some of the assigned stuff since you were nominated, but I don't want the rest of the week to be awful for you."

"It's not awful," I said. "Really. Jacob, Callie, Eric, and I just need to keep our distance from each other and we'll be okay."

Paige walked over and wrapped her arms around me. I hugged her back, glad that we'd smoothed most of everything over and also relieved that things weren't going to be weird before fall break. I didn't want to start off fall break with Paige and I being awkward around each other. I had enough people to worry about.

"We need to totally start planning everything we're going to do over break soon," I said.

"Absolutely," Paige said. "We so have to."

We smiled at each other and I willed the week to hurry and be over already.

When I got to history class later that afternoon, I took my seat and my eyes shifted between Jacob and Eric, who were already in there.

Eric had his phone under his desk and was texting. A lot. His phone buzzed seconds after he sent a text and he kept texting. He was slouched in his seat in a black T-shirt and jeans. Every few seconds, he'd grin, then type something back.

Then I looked over at Jacob. He sat at his desk, not even looking up. He looked as if he hadn't slept for days and he just stared at the front of the classroom as if he didn't know why he was there or what was going on. I watched him and my head started to pound. He had to be upset about breaking up with Callie, but I also knew it was about me. He'd wanted us to be together and he'd thought that would happen immediately after he'd left Callie.

But I'd made it clear at the bonfire that it couldn't

happen. Not now. Not ever. He hadn't believed me, but I'd have to do everything I could to convince him that I wanted to be single. That I didn't want him back. That we couldn't be together.

But part of my brain went to *that* place. What if I waited long enough, however long that was, and we did try to be boyfriend and girlfriend? *No.* I pushed the thoughts away. I'd decided to stay single and if we got back together now, it might make Callie question my story from the night of my party. That couldn't happen. I never wanted her to hate Jacob. I'd rather she hated me instead.

I sat through history class, not saying a word, and was sure that would be the most awkward class of my day. But when I got to math class, I saw Callie dressed in jeans and a red T-shirt. She was *really* down if she didn't dress up for Spirit Day.

I walked by her and took my seat, forcing myself not to go up to her. I couldn't. It would blow everything. But it hurt to watch my former BFF be teary through our entire class. I didn't know how many of those classes I could take.

18

RAH, RAH, RAH

CLASSES FINALLY ENDED FOR THE DAY AND I headed with the rest of the seventh and eighth graders to the gym for the pep rally. I'd almost bailed, but I knew I'd get detention from Headmistress Drake if she found out I'd skipped without a reason.

I climbed the bleachers with Paige and we sat next to each other. Paige's cheeks were flushed and she had a tiny green and gold flag in her right hand.

"This is sooo cool," she said. "Yay, Canterwood!" I chewed on the inside of my lip so I didn't say anything about how she was already cheering before the pep rally even started. I remembered my words from this morning— I wanted the rest of Homecoming to be awesome for Paige. She deserved it.

I stared down at my black sandals, then looked up when the Trio climbed the bleachers and entered our row. They passed Paige and Heather sat by me with Julia and Alison by her side.

"Pep rally," Heather said. "Yay."

I laughed at how flat her "yay" was.

"I know," I said. "Yay."

We laughed, and beside Heather, Alison rolled her eyes. She leaned past us and looked at Paige. "*I'm* excited," she said. "This is so cool!"

"I know!" Paige said, smiling. "The pep rally is going to kick off the final big events of the week. It's going to be awesome."

Heather and I shared a glance. The next day and a half weren't going to be awesome for us, but at least our friends were excited.

I breathed a quiet sigh of relief when Ryan walked up the bleachers and sat by Paige. She grinned at him and he couldn't stop looking at her.

Whew. At least I was off I-love-Homecoming-so-so-much duty. Ryan was as into it as Paige, so he'd fill in for me. I could spend the rest of the period mocking the pep rally with Heather, and Paige wouldn't notice.

I was about to turn to Heather, when I saw Callie enter

the gym and climb into the second row of stands. She looked devastated. Her eyes were pink and she had her lips pressed together. I wished I could do *something*, but I knew there wasn't a thing I could do.

Part of me was almost furious with Jacob for doing that to Callie. He'd hurt her and she was my former best friend. But I couldn't hate Jacob. I couldn't be mad at him for staying with someone when he didn't feel anything. That would have been leading Callie on. I just wished that they would have been happy together and that it would have been enough.

I tore my eyes away from Callie and saw Heather watching me. She didn't say anything, but I could tell she wanted to.

We both watched as Eric walked through the gym doors with Rachel and her posse. The more I watched Rachel, the more I realized it looked like she was the Heather of seventh grade, only nicer. Rachel and her friends sat on the bottom row of the bleachers and they were practically bouncing in their seats.

"They should have been cheerleaders," Heather grumbled.

"No kidding," I said.

Another wave of students came inside and Jacob

followed the group. He climbed up a few rows and by the look on his face, he was as thrilled to be here as I was.

The gym lights started flashing on and off and the Canterwood cheerleaders ran into the center of the court, shaking their pom-poms. A Billboard chart top hit started playing and the girls did back-flips and tossed each other into the air. The crowd started screaming and cheering as the cheerleaders finished their routine with a pyramid. I applauded along with everyone else, but my clapping was robotic.

The lights went down and the cheerleaders left the floor. In the dim lighting, I saw people hurry onto the floor and crouch down. An infectious beat starting playing and the lights flashed on. Canterwood's dance team jumped up and started a hip-hop number that got everyone to their feet. Members of the spirit club ran around the edge of the field and tossed balled up Canterwood Crest T-shirts into different sections of the stands.

The rest of the pep rally was a blur. The flashing lights, the music, and the dancing were almost overwhelming. All I could think about was getting out of here and going back to the safety of my room. The lights finally came on and Headmistress Drake, microphone in hand, walked to the center of the floor.

"Thank you, students!" Headmistress Drake said. I'd never heard her so excited. "I hope you all enjoyed the pep rally and are ready for our upcoming game. With all of you to cheer on the team, I'm sure Canterwood Crest Academy will emerge victorious! Go Canterwood!"

She left the floor to applause and I leaned down to grab my bag. When I looked back up, Callie was already bolting across the floor. She was one of the first ones out the door. I fought back the tightness that was choking my throat. Callie had just lost me at my party. And now she was without Jacob.

19

THE 411
ON JASMINE

AFTER THE PEP RALLY, I RACED BACK TO
Winchester to change so I wouldn't be late for my lesson. I tugged on breeches and a T-shirt and pulled my
hair into a messy ponytail before running for the stable.
I grabbed Charm's tack from the tack room and headed
for his stall.

I smiled when I saw Charm's head poking over the
stall door.

"Hey, boy," I said. "I missed you."

I kissed his muzzle and he nudged my shoulder. He
stepped back and I unlatched his stall door. I grabbed his
halter and led him out of his stall and to a pair of crossties. I clipped them on and opened his trunk to grab his
tack box.

"Let's get you sparkling and then we'll go to our lesson," I said.

Charm bobbed his head, moving the crossties up and down.

His coat wasn't dirty since he hadn't been outside, so I picked up a body brush and flicked it over his neck, back, and hindquarters.

I took his saddle pad from on top of his trunk and placed it over his back, smoothing out any wrinkles. I hoisted the saddle into the air and put it on top of the saddle pad, then tightened the girth.

Charm stood still as I unclipped the crossties and let them drop to the ground. I put the reins over his head and adjusted his bridle in my hands. He opened his mouth when I placed the snaffle bit between his lips and pulled the crownpiece over his ears. After I buckled his bridle, I picked up my helmet and fastened it.

"Ready?" I asked him. Together, we walked down the aisle to the outdoor arena. Mr. Conner had sent Heather and me an e-mail this afternoon and had told us to meet him outside. I mounted Charm just before he walked through the entrance. We warmed up along the rail and Heather and Aristocrat joined us minutes later.

Heather rode Aristocrat next to me and shook her

head. "I'd rather ride without stirrups for the rest of my life than attend another pep rally," she said.

"Me too. And we both know how much we hate that."

We both sighed and let our horses into trots. We warmed them up until Mr. Conner came, and then we halted them in front of him.

"Hi, Heather," Mr. Conner said, nodding at her. "Sasha." He looked at me. "I want to work on flatwork today, so why don't you move your horses out to the rail at a sitting trot and we'll get started."

Charm's trot was smooth as we moved to the wall and I had no trouble not bouncing in the saddle. We made a couple of laps around the arena before Mr. Conner signaled to us to canter. I squeezed my knees against Charm's sides and he jumped forward. I remembered how Mr. Conner had praised Heather for not letting Charm rush, so I pulled him back to a trot. I made him do another lap at the slower pace before I gave him the signal to canter. This time, he moved smoothly from one gait to the next.

"Nice decision, Sasha," Mr. Conner said. "Smart to pull him back and then ask him to canter. I was hoping you'd do just that."

I hid my smile. Compliments from Mr. Conner were rare and I was glad he'd noticed that I'd made the decision to slow Charm, even if it meant not keeping pace with Heather and Aristocrat.

"Cross over the center and reverse directions, please," Mr. Conner called.

Charm and I followed Heather and Aristocrat across the center of the arena and started cantering in the opposite direction. Charm seemed to pay more attention to me than he had before I'd stopped him. He kept one ear back in my direction, listening for any cues.

"Good boy," I said.

"Sasha," Mr. Conner called. "Try not to talk to Charm so much."

I closed my mouth and nodded.

We trotted for a few more minutes before Mr. Conner held up his hand. "I want you head to the other end of the arena and you'll take turns cantering your horses through the poles. They're spaced far enough apart that you can do a medium canter and be safe."

Heather and I let Charm and Aristocrat walk to the opposite end of the arena. Charm stretched his neck as he walked and huffed. Maybe he wished I rode Western instead of English—he definitely loved it when we did Western-style exercises and I could see him winning pole-bending competitions.

"You can go first," Heather said, nodding at the course.

"Thanks," I said.

Heather stopped Aristocrat away from the beginning of the course and I circled Charm at a trot, then a canter.

"Don't let him rush," Mr. Conner said.

I tightened my fingers around the reins. "I won't."

I let Charm out of the circle and headed for the first pole. He yanked his head forward and tried to pull the reins through my fingers. He was getting too excited before we even started. I pushed my weight into the saddle with my seat and heels, trying to slow him.

Charm reacted to my movement and eased to a slower canter. I started to say, "Good job," but remembered Mr. Conner's words from earlier. I'd reward Charm after our lesson if he kept doing well.

He cantered to the pole until it felt that he was going to slam into it before I shifted my weight to the side and tugged on the right rein. In an instant, Charm shifted to the side. His canter stayed smooth as he bent around the pole and we were so close to it that my boot almost brushed against the plastic.

Charm swerved in the next direction, barely needing me to tell him what to do. He saw the poles and he just went for it. *But you still need to keep control of him,* I thought.

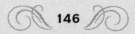

If I didn't, his well-paced canter would turn into a gallop and it could get dangerous.

Charm dashed through the six poles and I kept myself balanced in the saddle and made sure I didn't tip or tilt as he changed direction. He curved around the final pole and I let him canter four strides toward the end of the arena before slowing him to a trot, then a walk. I patted his neck and turned him back to face Heather and Mr. Conner.

"Nice work, Sasha," Mr. Conner said, nodding at me. "You knew Charm would have a tendency to dash through the poles, but you kept control of him. He looked supple as he moved through the poles."

"Thank you," I said. I stopped Charm next to Aristocrat and the horses didn't look away from each other—they stood and awaited instruction.

Mr. Conner flipped to a clean sheet of paper in his notebook and motioned to Heather.

"Heather, you may go when you're ready," Mr. Conner said.

Heather pushed down her heels and settled into the saddle. It was all too easy to fall off to the side if a rider wasn't prepared for pole bending. I thought back to the first time I'd tried it at my old stable. Charm, still very green, had rushed through the course and I hadn't been prepared when we'd taken the first pole. Charm had leaned so far over that I'd tipped off to the side, tumbled out of the saddle and bruised my shoulder.

Heather led Aristocrat into a trot, then a canter. The chestnut's tail streamed out behind him as he cantered and he looked sleek enough to skim around all of the poles. Heather's plum-colored shirt flashed as Aristocrat's body curved around the first pole and they reached the second pole faster than Charm and I had. They darted back and forth through the poles and I couldn't help but be impressed with how fast they completed the course. Not only were they seconds faster than Charm and me, but Heather also got Aristocrat closer to each pole.

"Nice," I said as Heather pulled Aristocrat up beside Charm and me.

Heather cocked her head. "I think that was better than 'nice.'"

Mr. Conner scribbled something on his chart and walked over to us.

"Well done, Heather," he said. "Aristocrat's agility is in his build, but it's also from the hard work you've put into getting him there. I'm impressed with how close you came to each pole without touching it. Excellent job."

"Thanks," Heather said.

Mr. Conner looked at both of us. "Let's amp up the difficulty of the lesson."

Heather and I glanced at each other.

"Drop your stirrups and cross them over your saddle," Mr. Conner said. "I want you to do the exercise again at a slow canter."

That was going to be a little more difficult. Heather and I kicked our feet out of the stirrups and crossed them.

Mr. Conner nodded to me and I let Charm into a slow canter. I gripped with my knees and wrapped my fingers around Charm's mane to help keep my balance. I held Charm at an easy canter and he listened. He moved around the first pole and I shifted to stay in the saddle. Charm kept an even pace and didn't rush between the poles. I stayed focused on keeping my balance and moving Charm through the course. I fought back a smile when we finished and turned to face Heather and Mr. Conner.

Heather completed the course and her second ride was almost better than her first. She rode the course in a way that almost made me want to take notes.

"Heather," Mr. Conner said. "You made it appear as if you were riding *with* stirrups. Your balance is superb and you sit tight in the saddle without gripping Aristocrat too hard."

"Thank you," Heather said.

Everything he'd said to her was true—it really had been a great ride.

"That was an excellent lesson, girls," Mr. Conner said. "Take good care of your horses and see you next class." Heather and I dismounted and started walking the horses side by side.

"So I heard Jasmine is back at Wellington," Heather said after Mr. Conner was out of the arena.

"You did?" I asked. "How?"

Heather shook her head. "Do you not know me at all? I have connections—duh."

"How'd she get back in? Is she riding? Did she get in trouble there?"

"God, Silver," Heather said. "I didn't say I had *every* little detail. I just know she's back at Wellington and riding. That's it."

"Grrreat," I muttered. "Exactly what we need. She hates us and she's riding again. How did she get back on the riding team after she got expelled from Canterwood?"

"Who cares how she did it—it just matters that she did. We can't ease up even for one lesson."

"We'll definitely see her at shows—you know it." I sighed.

But Heather grinned. "I'm counting on it."

20

KNIGHTS VS. PANTHERS

LATER IN THE DAY, I WALKED TO A PART OF campus I *never* visited—the football field. Almost everyone was wearing a green and gold jersey or something in school colors. I'd put on a green T-shirt and jeans. That was as far as I was willing to go. My brain had worked through every possible excuse to get out of coming to the game, but because I was a—gag—*nominee*, I had to go.

And not just go. But sit in a special section with other people who'd been nominated. Callie. Jacob. Eric. Me. Paige. Heather. Nicole. Troy. Ben. Ryan.

As the eighth-grade nominees, we'd all have to sit in the same section.

I had to force myself to keep walking toward the field. I'd promised Paige to meet her and Ryan near the entrance. The closer I got, the louder things were. I was almost overwhelmed by the noise and volume of people on campus.

I reached the entrance to the football field and looked around for Paige and Ryan. There were so many people, I wondered if I'd have to text her to find her. Then, I saw her.

"Paige," I called.

She turned and her eyes scanned the crowed. I waved and she saw me. She smiled and waved back. Her other hand held Ryan's.

"You look so great," I said. Paige looked supercute in a tight-fitting Canterwood football jersey, skinny jeans, and flip-flops. Her hair was in a high ponytail and she'd curled the ends—very cheerleader-esque.

"Thanks!" Paige turned her cheek to me and pointed. "Like it?"

I couldn't help but smile. She had CCA painted in green on her cheek in the school's font.

"Love," I said.

"She tried to get me to have my face painted," Ryan said, grinning. "But I passed."

"Understandable," I said. "But Paige can be *very* persuasive, so watch out. You might walk out of here tonight with face paint."

Paige and Ryan both smiled.

"Let's grab food and then find our seats," Paige said. "Okay?"

Ryan and I nodded.

I followed them and couldn't help but be just a tiny bit excited. Paige's enthusiasm was infectious tonight and if I was careful, I could probably avoid Callie, Jacob, and Eric and just hang with Paige, Ryan, Heather, and the rest of the nominees tonight. Besides, it was a football game. No one talked much during those things, right?

We got in line at the concession stand and the line moved surprisingly fast. We ordered corn dogs, giant sodas, and waffle fries. Paige looked around the stands, then pointed.

"I think we're supposed to sit in that box," she said. "Let's go see."

Ryan and I followed her and we climbed the bleachers until we reached a skybox that was roped off. RESERVED FOR EIGHTH-GRADE JUNIOR ROYAL COURT NOMINEES, read a sign.

"That's us!" Paige said. "Omigod, I can't believe we're sitting *here*."

Ryan unclipped the rope, letting us go into the stands first. I flashed back to when he'd first *really* smiled at

Paige—when he'd played a bodyguard at her *Teen Cuisine* party and had undone the velvet rope to let us into the room. I couldn't help but be happy when I watched Paige with Ryan. She was animated and excited—not at all nervous and awkward like she'd been when they'd first started getting to know each other.

We were the first ones in the stands. I picked the last seat in the back of the second row. Paige sat beside me, Ryan went next to her so at least I knew that no one could sit by me or behind me. I was glad we'd gotten here a little early.

I started eating my fries and watched Ryan dip a fry in ketchup and offer it to Paige. She took it and did the same for him. I felt a twinge of loneliness. I missed Eric's friendship—the way he'd been there for me and how good he'd made me feel. Sometimes, I missed his support. But then I looked at Paige and Ryan—how it wasn't just a friendship. They *like*-liked each other. I wanted that. With Jacob.

But it doesn't matter, I reminded myself. I forced myself to eat another fry. *Drama-free life means no guys for a while.*

Heather walked into the booth and sat in front of me. "Hey," she said, turning around. My eyes landed on her cheek. She had a tiny football painted there.

"Omigod," I said, covering a laugh. "What did you do?"

"Julia and Alison made me." Heather rolled her eyes. "I totally didn't want to, but they forced me."

I liked making her squirm for once. "Julia and Alison," I said slowly, "made *you* do something?"

"Silver, I'm going to push you out of the skybox if you don't shut up," Heather said, smiling sweetly.

"Okay, okay." I held up my hands.

Troy and Ben, two of the other guy nominees, walked past us and took seats at the end of the row. They turned around and said hi to Paige, Ryan, and me. I said hi back, but let Paige and Ryan carry the chatter about the football game. I didn't even know what team we were playing.

I ate my corn dog and watched as the stands started to fill. I looked up when someone walked past me and headed for an empty seat by Troy.

Eric. He had a Canterwood Crest baseball hat on and it shielded his eyes. He greeted Troy and Ben with a fist bump. I gripped the stick of my corn dog, almost paralyzed with wondering if he was going to turn around.

He shifted his head back and saw Ryan, Paige, and then me. "Hey," he said. His voice was calm and his face showed nothing—he seemed completely cool sitting in the skybox with his ex-girlfriend. Paige and Ryan nodded back at him; I looked away and put my plate under my seat. I wasn't hungry anymore.

Nicole, bubbly as always, walked inside and sat beside Eric.

"Can you *believe* we're at Homecoming?!" Nicole said.

"I know!" Paige said.

"And we're sitting in the skybox!" Alison said.

Heather turned around and fake-choked herself. That made me smile.

"That's *exactly* how I feel," I said so only Heather could hear. I stuck out my tongue and rolled my eyes. We both laughed and I closed my mouth when I saw Callie walking up the stairs to our seating.

Callie looked at me, then glanced at Heather. Like Eric, her face was a mask. Her brown eyes gave away nothing and she didn't even blink at seeing us laugh together. She plopped into the seat in front of me and stared out at the football field. It *had* to be as uncomfortable for her as it was for me. She was sitting next to Heather and in front of me. Heather turned back around and both girls sat as far away from each other as they could in their chairs.

The talking in the skybox grew quieter. Then everyone fell silent when *he* reached the rope. I dropped my eyes to my lap. Jacob entered the back row of the skybox and

walked past me and everyone else to take the last seat at the end of the aisle.

I'd been delusional to think I'd be able to enjoy this for even a second. Even in the open space, I felt like I couldn't breathe with Jacob sitting seats away from me and Callie in front of me.

"Good evening, everyone."

Headmistress Drake stepped into the skybox and smiled at all of us.

I tried to smile back, but couldn't.

"I'm glad to see all of you here and representing our school," Headmistress Drake said. She'd pinned a CCA pin to her ivory button-up blouse.

"I hope you enjoy your seats from the skybox. Congratulations on your nominations, and please enjoy the game."

She smiled at us before walking out of our seating and heading toward the spaces reserved for faculty.

I felt trapped in the skybox, so I forced myself to focus on something else. The Canterwood Crest football team lined up on the side of the field. The giant overhead lights illuminated the players and the coach. The team jogged in place and waited as a paper Canterwood Crest banner was held in front of them.

I glanced away from the field and looked down the

aisle to Jacob. I couldn't see him around everyone else.

You don't need to see Jacob, I told myself. *Watch the game.*

The PA system crackled on and the crowd became silent.

"Are you ready?" the announcer asked, his voice booming over the field. I looked up and could see a guy in a tiny announcer's box overlooking the field. He had on giant headphones and his face was close to a microphone.

Everyone screamed and clapped.

"That wasn't loud enough," the announcer said. "I'm asking you again. Are. You. Ready?"

"Yeah!" The crowd screamed in unison. People whistled and clapped. I looked to the other side of the field and saw green and gold flags and pom-poms waving. In a much smaller section, visiting students from nearby Pershing Prep raised their red and black flags in support of their team. But they were on Canterwood turf and we outnumbered them. Big time.

On the side of the field, our players were getting ready. They flexed their arms, straightened their helmets and bumped fists with each other. The Canterwood cheerleaders assembled at our end of the field and started chanting.

"Go, Canterwood, go! Go, Canterwood, go!" they screamed.

Heather and I glanced at each other and shook our heads.

At the opposite end, Pershing Prep's cheerleaders chanted for their school.

"Pershing Prep panthers!" the girls screamed.

The Pershing Prep cheerleaders were soon drowned out by the home crowd.

Two Canterwood cheerleaders unrolled a giant Canterwood Crest Academy paper banner and held it ready for our players to rush through it. The mascots—a panther and our knight—entered the field and started rousing the crowd. Everyone got to their feet.

"Please welcome the Canterwood Crest Academy kniiiights!" the announcer said.

"Yeah! Woo!" Paige screamed, clapping her hands.

Our players ran forward and broke through the banner. They jogged away from the entrance so the Panthers' cheerleaders could assemble their school's banner. The Panthers ran through their banner and we all sat back in our seats. I forced myself to keep my eyes on the players—I needed something to look at instead of who was sitting with me in the skybox.

21

GAME OVER

IT TOOK EIGHT HOURS JUST TO GET TO halftime. Okay, okay, so that wasn't totally true, but it felt like that long. When the players left the field and Canterwood's cheerleaders back flipped and cartwheeled onto the grass, Heather turned around.

"I need a soda," she said.

"Me too," I said quickly.

I looked over at Paige to tell her I'd be back, but she was cheering for the show. She probably wouldn't even notice that I was gone.

I hurried past Callie and followed Heather down the steps and to a concession stand on our side of the field.

We got in line and Heather turned to me. "Don't do that. You didn't do anything to break up Callie and Jacob.

He made a move on you—anyone with a brain would know that."

I shot her a look. "Well, no one but Paige *does* know, so shut up. I don't want Callie to find out. It would hurt her too much."

Heather stared at me and folded her arms.

"What?" I asked.

"You're not protecting Callie anymore."

"Yes, I am! Why else would I let this go on and not be able to be her friend?"

We moved closer to the stand and Heather sighed. "Silver, don't act like I'm dumb. You don't want Jacob to look bad. It's obvious."

I opened my mouth, trying to think of what to say. She was right, like she always was, but I didn't want to tell her that. Heather's phone rang.

She pulled it out of her pocket, frowning when she looked at the caller ID.

"Hi," she said.

Her voice was unusually high. She paused and covered her other ear with her hand.

"The noise?" Heather's face turned pink. "Oh, I'm walking by a football game on my way to the stable. I had my afternoon lesson, but I'm going back to ride."

Her dad—I knew it. He never let up on her about rid-ing. He was always after her about practicing more even though she spent more time at the stable than anyone. Even Mr. Conner had finally told Mr. Fox that his constant pres-sure on Heather wasn't helping, but he didn't let up. I'd walked in on Mr. Fox questioning a nearly teary Heather one day in the tack room and I'd stepped in and made it sound as if she did nothing but practice, which wasn't true anymore. She spent a *lot* of time at the stable, but she was also working on balancing that with other things.

"Yes, Dad," Heather said into the phone. "Mr. Conner said my ride during the lesson was perfect. I'm going back now to work with Aristocrat over a few jumps. I'm getting up early before class to ride, too. Like always."

Like as of weeks ago, I thought. Our afternoon lessons were so intense, there was no reason for us to get up before classes and ride. And Heather wasn't. But I stood quietly and looked away so that she didn't think I was listening to every word.

"I will, Dad," Heather said. "I'll call you after my les-son. Bye."

She snapped the phone shut with such force, I was sur-prised it didn't break. She rubbed her nose with her hand and took a long breath.

"You okay?" I asked.

She shrugged. "Whatever, totally. You know how my dad is about riding. If I told him I was at a football game, he'd freak."

"But you didn't have a choice. We *had* to come."

Heather laughed. "You try that on my dad. He'd call the headmistress to find out if it was true, which would be insanely embarrassing."

I nodded. "Yeah," I said softly. "It would be. Sorry."

"Forget about it."

I watched Heather out of the corner of my eye as we moved through the line. Her dad had rattled her. She was trying to be cool and act as if it didn't matter, but it did. I could see how she'd changed the second she'd looked at the caller ID.

We ordered sodas and walked back to the stands without saying a word. I passed Callie and she looked away when I walked by. I sat down and clutched my cup of soda. I *had* to say something to her about the breakup. She was hurting and I couldn't just sit here and watch her be in pain.

"Callie," I said, leaning toward her shoulder. I wanted to get it out before I overanalyzed every word.

She turned around, her black hair flipping over her shoulder. "Are you *talking* to me?"

Her tone almost made me wince, but I forced myself to keep talking. "I just wanted to say that I'm sorry about—"

Callie shook her head. "Oh, my God. Please. Don't even. I can't believe you'd start to say that."

"But I *am* sorry," I said.

Callie's brown eyes darkened. "I told you not to ever talk to me again. Leave me alone." She shrugged. "Besides, I give you twenty-four hours before you and Jacob are together. He's all yours—your birthday wish is granted."

I sat through the rest of the game and didn't move from my seat. Every so often, Paige, Ryan and other people in our skybox would jump up and scream.

Near the fourth quarter Paige reached over and touched my arm.

"You okay?" she asked. She almost had to yell the last word when the crowd screamed.

"Fine," I said. "Just tired."

Paige nodded and flicked her eyes to Callie's back. "I saw what you—"

I slashed my hand across my throat, cutting her off. "Not here," I said.

"Okay."

Paige looked back at the field.

I sat through the final minutes of the game, ignoring every tackle and field goal. I didn't even look at the score. I just watched the clock tick down the final minutes to when I could leave. Finally, the clock hit 00:00. The Canterwood crowd exploded with cheers.

"YESSS!" Paige screamed beside me.

"All right!!" Ryan yelled. Screams for our team rang out across the field and I finally looked at the scoreboard. We'd won by three points.

I grabbed my empty cup and slung my purse over my shoulder. I turned and looked down the row of seats.

Jacob was staring back at me.

22

HOMECOMING
FREAKOUT

BY THE TIME MS. UTZ'S HEALTH CLASS
started on Friday, the level of excitement over Homecoming had reached code red. I'd taken every side hallway
that existed to stay away from the noise and craziness.
Nobody seemed worried about getting to class on time—
everyone was talking in the hallway or texting. On a normal day, no one would even dare use a cell in the hall. It
seemed like all the rules disappeared today.

I walked to my desk and sat down, ignoring everyone
who was chattering nonstop about Homecoming.

"Omigod, can you believe the dance is tonight?" asked
one girl.

"Nooo!" said a girl sitting next to her. "There's so
much we have to do!" She flipped open a notebook and

stared down at a page of paper. "Manis, pedis, blowouts, tweezing . . ."

I turned away. This was *ridiculous*. Of course they were excited—they weren't being forced to go! The classroom started to fill up and I watched Eric, and then Jacob, walk inside. I didn't want to look at Jacob. I'd hurried out of the skybox last night after I'd caught him staring at me.

I paged through my health book, not even able to read the text. I couldn't concentrate with everyone talking at top volume. Paige came in and sat beside me, grinning.

"We should have had the day off," Paige said. "This is such a waste of time."

"Yeah. Totally."

"No one can concentrate. We're all focused on the dance!"

I just nodded. I was thinking about the dance, but my reasons were different from Paige's. I really didn't want to dampen her first big school event with Ryan, so I had to make an effort.

"Are you more freaked out or excited about the dance?" I asked.

Paige paused, smoothing her purple T-shirt. "Can it be equal?" she asked, smiling. "It's the first time I'll be dancing with Ryan and I'm so nervous. You know that I took dance lessons, but it's been a while. What if I've forgotten everything and I step on his feet or something?"

"You won't do that. You're a great dancer—Ryan will have to work to keep up with you."

Paige's tense shoulders relaxed. "And you'll help me with clothes and makeup, right?"

"Given!"

Ms. Utz walked into the room. Usually the talking would cease and everyone would wait for her to take attendance. But today, the noise level stayed the same.

"Class," Ms. Utz said, looking up from her notebook. "Let's stop the talking now. We're about to start."

The loud talking turned to quiet chatting. Ms. Utz started to take attendance, but the whispers didn't stop.

"Excuse me," Ms. Utz said. Her voice was stern. "I realize that it's the last day before fall break and the dance is tonight. However, this does not permit you to continue to talk when class has started."

Now everyone fell silent.

"Thank you," Ms. Utz said. She went back to taking attendance. I tuned her out and went back to thinking about the football game. I had to have been caught up in the moment and pumped up by the craziness around me. I *did not* want to date Jacob. I didn't even want to

be thinking about him! But then why did my chest feel crushed whenever he looked at me?

I had to stay away from him—*faaar* away from him. Especially during tonight's Homecoming. We'd be forced to hang out together for a while for junior royal court stuff, but I'd stay by Paige and away from him.

Ms. Utz finished taking attendance. She flipped through her teacher's guide and settled on a page. "Let's go over the final chapter about first aid for cuts and burns, then we'll talk about homework during break."

"Paige," she said. "Please start reading at the top of page ninety."

Paige started reading aloud and I made myself take notes as she read. I needed anything to distract me from thinking about tonight.

When I got to theater class, I looked for Heather. I'd made up my mind that I wasn't going to even so much as glance at Jacob. I was too afraid that people were already expecting me to be with Jacob. They probably thought we'd gotten together the second he'd left Callie. We had to keep distance between us as much as possible.

I spotted Heather sitting in the front row and I walked down the main aisle to her row. The theater lights felt

harsh at this distance from the stage and I felt like a spot-light was on me.

"Omigod," I said, falling into the chair beside Heather. "Last class for an entire week."

She rubbed her forehead. "I know. And it's the last day of Homecoming. If it had lasted any longer, I would have locked myself in my room until it was over or something."

"Me too. We just have to get through the dance and then we've made it."

Heather nodded. "I just want to go riding and pretend the dance isn't happening."

"Agreed."

And as excited as I was about this being my last class for an entire week, I hadn't let myself think about break yet. Things with Paige were still a tiny bit off and if I thought about spending the week with her, I started to worry about things getting weird if she asked me about the party or if I had any interest in trying to be with Jacob. I glanced quickly behind me to see if he was here yet. He was sitting two rows behind me and a few seats over. I turned my attention back to the stage.

Ms. Scott walked up the stairs and stood at center stage. She wore her trademark red lipstick and her black hair was pulled into a half updo. "You all aren't thinking about, I don't know, the dance tonight, are you?"

Everyone laughed.

"I'm not the kind of teacher who assigns homework over a break," Ms. Scott said. "How is it a break if you're working?"

"Exactly!" a girl a few seats down from Heather said.

Ms. Scott smiled. "It's the last class of the day and as my 'happy fall break' gift, I'm letting you go now. I'm sure you've got lots of things you'd like to do before the dance, so go."

The class started cheering and clapping. Even Heather and I smiled at each other. Who cared *why* class was canceled—at least it was!

"Have a fun, safe break and see you all soon," Ms. Scott said.

I was out of my seat before she finished her last word. Heather followed me up the aisle and I almost broke into a jog to get out of the theater before Jacob could try to talk to me or something.

"I'm definitely *not* using the extra time to get ready for the dance," Heather said. "I've got my riding clothes in my bag, so I'm changing and riding before our lesson."

"Totally thinking the same," I said. "Maybe the stable will be quiet since lessons were optional today."

Heather snorted. "No one's going to show today. We'll be the only people there when lessons start—you know it."

Mr. Conner had sent an e-mail this morning and had said lessons were optional for all students who wanted to use the extra time to pack for a trip home if they were going off campus for fall break or to get ready for the end of Homecoming. There was no way either Heather or I would miss a lesson—especially not one for the YENT.

The farther away we got from the theater building, the more I relaxed. Jacob wasn't coming after me to talk and Callie was still in class.

We walked into the stable and the main aisle was deserted. It was so weird to be here without the usual crowd.

"Are Julia and Alison riding after class?" I asked.

"They better ride since they just got their privileges back, but they're being crazy about Homecoming, so I don't know."

We changed in the bathroom and got our horses' tacks. I smiled at Charm as I walked down the aisle toward his stall. His head was hanging over the door and he pointed his ears at me as I approached.

"Hi, guy," I said. I put down his tack and reached up to

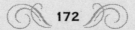

run my hand down his blaze. "I'm glad we get to hang out more together before I go to Paige's for break."

I unlatched his stall door, clipped a lead line to his halter and led him out. I put him on crossties closest to his stall and got his tack box from my trunk. I wanted to take my time grooming him—he deserved extra attention since I'd be away for a week. But I trusted Mike and Doug to take excellent care of him and Charm loved them both.

I grabbed Charm's hoof pick and ran my hand down his leg, squeezing above the fetlock. He raised his hoof and I scraped out what little muck had accumulated since yesterday. After his hooves were clean, I brushed him until he was super shiny. His chestnut coat gleamed softly under the overhead lights and from the sunlight that came in through the windows.

I tacked him up, thinking about how Heather was probably about ready to come find me to see what was taking so long. I snapped on my helmet and we started toward the indoor arena. It was too hot to ride outside right now.

"What took you so long?" Heather asked when I led Charm inside. She rolled her eyes as she rode Aristocrat over.

"I wanted to spend more time with him," I said. "I'm going to miss him over break."

Heather nodded and the attitude disappeared from her face. "I get that." She reached down and patted Aristocrat's neck. "I'm going to miss him too. But it's only for a week. When we get back, we'll practically be living in the stable to get ready for the schooling show."

"That's true." I smiled. "We'll be back for a day and we'll start complaining about the schedule."

Heather rolled her eyes. "You know it."

I let Charm into a trot and we moved toward the arena wall. Heather followed behind us on Aristocrat and I dropped my shoulders, which had inched toward my ears all day because of the stress about tonight. I busied myself with thinking about something else I had to do: pack. I'd been ignoring it all week as my relationship with Paige went up and down. Tonight was important—I didn't want anything to go wrong at the dance—especially the night before I went to Paige's for a week.

"Drop your hands, Silver," Heather said. "You look ridiculous."

Oops. My hands were at chest level. I settled them over Charm's neck.

We worked through a solid warm-up and coached each other while we waited for our lesson to start.

"Aristocrat's head seems high," I said.

Heather nodded once, then corrected him. Aristocrat lowered his chin the second she asked him to.

I almost couldn't believe what we were doing—if we'd tried to critique each other weeks ago, we would have torn each other apart. We still weren't really friends, but our relationship had definitely changed.

I looked up, surprised, when Mr. Conner entered the arena. I glanced up at the wall clock near the skybox—Heather and I had been practicing for more than half an hour. We'd been working so well together that it felt like we'd just gotten started.

"I had a feeling you'd both be here," Mr. Conner said, smiling. "I sincerely appreciate your dedication to the team. You both continue to impress me."

I held back a grin.

"Thanks," Heather and I said.

"Today's going to be a little different," Mr. Conner said. Heather and I looked over as Mike led a tacked-up Lexington into the arena. He handed Mr. Conner a helmet, which Mr. Conner put on and then mounted Lexington.

"For the first half of the lesson, you two are going to stay in the center of the arena and you'll critique *me*."

Heather and I looked at each other—confused. Mr. Conner was a top-level rider and there was no way we'd find anything wrong with his riding. We weren't even close to being experienced enough to give him feedback.

Mr. Conner looked at our faces and grinned. "I'm not going to ride in my normal style. I'm going to start with some obvious mistakes and I want you to point those out. As we go, my mistakes will become more and more subtle. You'll have to work harder to find them."

It sounded fun to be able to critique Mr. Conner instead of him always pointing out where we needed to improve.

"Any questions?" he asked.

Heather and I shook our heads.

"All right," Mr. Conner said. "Let's get started."

Heather and I moved Charm and Aristocrat to the center of the arena, swapping places with Mr. Conner. He guided Lexington along the wall and my eyes swept over his body, looking for mistakes.

"Shoulders down and back," Heather said. Mr. Conner listened to her and I focused, determined to find the next mistake. I watched as Lexington, still young and inexperienced, took advantage of the extra rein Mr. Conner gave him.

"Tighten your reins," I called. "He's drifting because no one's keeping him in line."

Mr. Conner tightened the reins and guided Lexington back along the wall.

It was getting tougher now. Heather and I both watched him, looking for some mistake.

"Elbows in," Heather called. I looked closer and noticed she was right. Mr. Conner tucked his elbows closer to his body.

He let Lexington into a trot and immediately, I knew something was off.

"You're—" Heather and I started at the same time.

She motioned to me.

"You're on the wrong diagonal," I said.

Mr. Conner sat for a beat, then started posting—this time on the correct diagonal.

Heather and I called him on a few more errors before he drew Lexington to a walk.

"How did you feel about that exercise?" he asked, halting the gray in front of us.

"It was different to see things from your perspective," I said. "You're watching a lot when we're riding and I never thought about that part of it before."

Heather adjusted her reins. "I thought it was helpful to see someone else make mistakes—some we do and don't even realize it—and to see how that would look to a judge."

"Exactly," Mr. Conner said. He reached down and

rubbed Lexington's neck. "That's what I was hoping for—I wanted you to see what the judges witness when they watch you and others ride. At this point in your riding careers, you rarely, if at all, exhibit any of the early mistakes I made. That's how it should be. As lessons for the YENT continue, we'll keep working on the finesse of your riding."

He smiled at us. "All right. Back to *me* critiquing you. Space out your horses and start spirals at a trot."

I trotted Charm to the left end of the arena and started maneuvering him through the pattern. My mind was focused on our ride—we had a show after fall break and I wasn't about to waste one second of our lesson.

We completed a few spirals before Mr. Conner held up his hand.

"Halt and I'll explain what we're going to do next," he said.

Heather and I stopped our horses in front of him, ready for instructions.

"I want to practice leg yields," Mr. Conner said. "We haven't worked on them since last year, so I want to remind you how to execute them."

I took a breath to keep down my nerves.

"Even if you don't intend to specialize in dressage,"

Mr. Conner said, "knowing how to do leg yields is a valuable tool for jumping. If you approach a jump at the wrong angle, a leg yield can help straighten your horse before he reaches the jump. Also, for pleasure riding, you can use leg yields to move to the side of a trail or to make opening and closing gates easier."

I nodded at that. Sometimes I had to dismount to open or close a gate. If I could do better leg yields, I'd be able to stay in the saddle.

"For this lesson, we'll refresh our memory about how to leg yield by doing it at a walk," Mr. Conner said. "Practice this on your own in between lessons and we'll eventually work up to doing it at a canter."

We nodded and I made a mental note to watch a few clips of leg yields on MyTube later.

"Heather," Mr. Conner continued. "I'd like you to go first. Ask Aristocrat to walk forward, then move him toward the wall. He should naturally want to walk along the wall since that's how we work during lessons. But don't allow him to turn completely—just bend."

Heather nodded. "Okay. And once he starts to bend, I'll ask him to move sideways while still going forward."

"Exactly," Mr. Conner said. "Let's see you try it."

Heather walked Aristocrat in a straight line, keeping

him away from the arena wall. Then she started to bend him toward the wall, and when he moved toward it, she pressed her boot against his side when he took another step forward. She also moved the inside rein with her hand and within two strides, Aristocrat began to move forward *and* sideways at the same time. They continued the movement for three strides before Heather turned him away from the wall and back to us.

"That was nice, Heather," Mr. Conner said. "How did you decide when Aristocrat had bent enough?"

Heather put the reins in one hand and pushed up her helmet. "I read an article in *Young Rider* about leg yields and I think it said the horse bent enough when you could see his nostril and eye."

Mr. Conner smiled. "That's correct. A great execution for the first attempt. Good job." He turned to me. "Your turn, Sasha. Remember not to pull on the reins—be gentle and ask Charm to flex to the side and not turn."

I nodded. "Okay."

But I didn't feel okay. It had been *so* long since I'd done leg yields—I worried that I'd forgotten everything and wouldn't be able to do it. I gave Charm rein to move forward because I knew the longer I sat still, the more I'd overanalyze and make myself and Charm more nervous.

I kept him straight for several strides before I flexed my fingers around the reins and asked him to bend just slightly. He started to make a complete turn, so I restraightened him and made him move forward for several more strides before asking him to bend again. This time, he moved slightly instead of a full turn. I timed pressing my leg against him when he moved his back leg forward.

C'mon, move sideways! I begged in my head.

It felt as if he wasn't going to do it and then he moved sideways and forward at the same time.

Yes!

I kept pressing and relaxing my leg against his side and I didn't make him take as many steps as Heather and Aristocrat had done. I patted his shoulder and we turned back to Mr. Conner and Heather.

Mr. Conner nodded at me. "Excellent, Sasha. Charm isn't as familiar with these movements as Aristocrat, but he listened to you and he worked hard at paying attention to what you were asking of him. Keep practicing it."

"We will," I said.

"Let's try that again," Mr. Conner said. He gestured at Heather. "Take Aristocrat though it at a walk."

I watched Heather start the exercise and I felt eager to

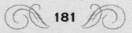

try again. When it was our turn, Charm seemed to know exactly what to do. He listened to me the first time and we completed the leg yield without making the same mistakes we had the first time. Mr. Conner made us practice for another half hour before he signaled us to bring our horses in front of him.

"Thank you, girls," he said. "That was a great lesson. Considering it's the day before fall break and the night of the dance, your rides were commendable. As a reward for your hard work, Mike and Doug will care for your horses."

"Thank you," Heather and I said.

"Enjoy the dance tonight and have a good break," Mr. Conner said. He grinned and pointed to his clipboard. "We'll *really* start working for the schooling show when you get back." He turned and walked out of the arena.

Heather and I dismounted and unsnapped our chin straps. We led the horses to the arena exit and toward the aisle to find Mike and Doug.

I saw Mike filling a bucket with water and he waved at us. "Be right there," he said. Heather and I nodded at him.

I rubbed Charm's neck, then hugged him. "I'm going to miss you, boy, but I'll be back in a week. And Mike and Doug always take great care of you."

Charm leaned against me, hugging me back. I buried

my face in his mane and held him tight before I let him go.

When I released him, I saw Heather lowering her arms from around Aristocrat's neck. Heather loved Aristocrat more than she let on and I knew she'd miss him just as much as I'd miss Charm.

Mike walked over and reached for their reins.

"Have a good break," he said. "I'll take good care of them."

"We know you will," I said. "And thanks."

Mike smiled and led Charm and Aristocrat down the aisle.

Heather pulled her hair out of its ponytail and shook it around her shoulders.

"I'm going back to my room," she said. "There's no way I'm going anywhere else—not with this craziness going on."

"Agreed," I said. "I'm putting in my earbuds until I get to my room. You know the second we walk out of here we'll hear a chant, or a cheer or something."

Heather laughed and we started down the aisle toward the exit. "For sure. If I hear 'Canterwood Crest is the best' one more time . . ."

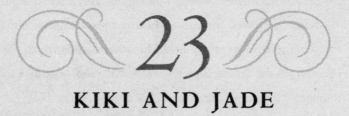

23

KIKI AND JADE

WHOA. I SURVEYED THE MESS THAT HAD ONCE been my room.

"Paige?" I called, stepping over a pile of flip-flops that looked as if they'd been tossed one by one from her closet. Her desk was covered with two curling irons, a flatiron, headbands, clips, and a half dozen brushes of different sizes.

"Sasha! Omigod, help!" Paige looked around her closet door. Her eyes were wide and her voice was squeaky.

"What's wrong?" I asked.

I stepped over the mess and pulled Paige out of her closet.

"I'm panicking! This is the Homecoming dance. With. Ryan. It's the biggest event of the fall and I have to look perfect."

"You *will* look amazing," I said. "We already picked out your dress and you looked gorgeous when you tried it on."

Paige picked up the hunter green dress off her bed. The one-shoulder dress skimmed above her knees and made her red hair look even more vibrant.

"But what if it looks horrible now?" Paige asked. She held it up to herself in front of the mirror.

"It won't. Put it on and you can wear a hoodie while we do your hair and makeup so we don't spill anything on your dress."

Paige took a deep breath. "Okay. I can do this."

While she changed, I plugged in a wide-barreled curling iron. Paige had wanted soft waves for tonight. I went through our makeup cases and picked a soft gray eye shadow for a smoky eye and black eyeliner for the corner of her eyelid. Soft, peachy blush would complement her pale skin and with a shimmery gloss, she'd look perfect for the dance. I busied myself with carefully selecting every product. Distraction was key.

I looked up from Paige's desk and she was eyeing herself in the mirror.

"See?" I asked. "The dress looks *beautiful*. I told you it would!"

Paige turned around, smiling. "It *does* look pretty good.

I was freaked that I'd hate it or something and then it would be too late to find another dress."

"Nope, you're wearing that. Done."

Paige laughed and saluted me. "Yes, ma'am."

I tossed her my pink hoodie and she zipped it up over her dress. She sat on her desk chair and I rubbed a light moisturizer over her cheeks. I could almost do her makeup on autopilot since we'd done each other's for several parties and events, but I wanted to stay focused on her.

I dabbed concealer under Paige's eyes and blended it into her skin. A light dusting of powder over her T-zone took away any shine and I grabbed a wide blush brush.

"This peach color always looks amazing on you," I said. "And wait till we use the eye shadow."

"But don't take too much time on me," Paige said. "You still have to shower, get dressed, and I've got to do your hair and makeup."

I waved my hand. "It's totally fine. I'm just going to run the flatiron through my hair after it's dry and it'll take seconds for me to put on my dress. Then the makeup's all you."

I was wearing a little black dress I'd bought over the summer for any semiformal occasion—I hadn't specifically picked it out for Homecoming.

I applied a thin line of black eyeliner to the outer corner of Paige's eyes and dusted her lids with eye shadow.

"Be right back," I told Paige. "I need the hair dryer."

"For what?" she asked, touching her hair. "It's already dry."

I plugged it in and held the eyelash curler under it. "Tell you in a sec."

I blasted the curler with heat for just a few seconds, then brought it back to Paige.

"I read in *TweenStyle* that if you heat the curler, it helps your lashes hold the curl longer."

"Ooh, cool."

I curled Paige's lashes and applied a light coat of mascara. After a careful application of barely-there pink gloss, she was ready.

I spun her chair to face the mirror so she could check her makeup.

"Is it okay?" I asked.

Paige's grin gave away her answer. "You're the best, Kiki."

I loved my makeup-artist name. I was always Kiki and Paige assumed the identity of Jade.

"Let's curl your hair and then I'll get dressed and Jade can do my makeup."

187

It took the curling iron only seconds to heat and I clipped Paige's long hair into sections. I carefully wrapped an inch-and-a-half–wide section of her hair around the barrel and let the clamp hold Paige's hair against the iron for a few seconds. I repeated the process through the rest of her hair, making gentle waves. When they'd cooled, I ran my fingers through them and separated them. They fell around Paige's shoulders, making her look sophisticated.

"Thank you so much!" Paige said. She grabbed a hand mirror and turned so she could see the back of her hair. "You're the best. I feel *so* much less nervous now."

"Good. I'm going to shower and get dressed, then you can do my makeup while my hair air dries a little."

I took a quick shower, towel dried my hair and pulled on my fuzzy purple robe. I sat in the designated makeup chair and let Jade get to work.

Paige knew how to do my makeup better than I did and I totally trusted her to do whatever she wanted.

"You don't even need foundation," Paige said. "I think tinted moisturizer and a little concealer will look great."

"Do it," I said. "You know what works."

Paige applied the moisturizer and dotted concealer under my eyes and on a zit that had popped up during the day. Ridic.

She pulled out liquid eyeliner and put a thin line on my top eyelid.

"Every time I try that," I said. "I always mess it up and have to start over."

"It's definitely harder to work with than a pencil," Paige said. "But the line is so clean—I love how it looks."

She brushed a shimmery silver eye shadow over my eyelids and coated my lashes with black mascara.

"Blush, gloss, and you're set," Paige said.

"Done," she announced a few minutes later. "You look so gorg."

I looked at myself in the mirror—my eyelids were a pretty silver-gray, my lips were coated with sheer pink gloss and light blush made my cheekbones stand out. My curled eyelashes looked flirty and I felt good, despite not wanting to go to the dance.

"Thanks, Jade," I said. "You never disappoint."

Paige smiled. "Go dry your hair and I'm going to try on just a few pairs of shoes. I still haven't really decided."

I shook my head, fake-mocking her. "You know you're wearing the black kitten heels."

"I *think* I'm wearing them. I have to try my other ones more time before I decide. What're you wearing?"

"Ballet flats," I said. "My silver ones."

I walked into the bathroom and took my time drying my hair. Wearing heels wasn't worth it since (a) I wasn't going to dance with anyone and (b) I wasn't going to hurt my feet for something I didn't care about.

Once my hair was dry, I pulled it into sections and flatironed it. It looked great now, but I crossed my fingers that it hadn't gotten humid out or my hair would go from smooth to frizz in five seconds.

I put on my dress and Paige smiled when she saw me.

"You look beautiful!" she said. "That cut is great on you and with ballet flats, you'll look superglam."

"Thanks. I'll probably ditch my purse for the silver clutch I ordered online last week."

Paige nodded. "Do it. It'll look great." She looked down at her feet. "And you were right. I went with the kitten heels."

"Knew it." I smiled.

I pulled essentials for the night—lip gloss, phone, compact, and keys—out of my big purse and stuffed them into my tiny clutch.

Paige and I did a final hair check and I tried to ignore the sick feeling in my stomach. This was going to be beyond awkward. I didn't want to stand onstage in the spotlight with Callie, Jacob, and Eric. It was bad enough that we were all forced to go to the dance, but I definitely didn't want to be that close to any of them. But it was going to be awkward for all of us. I sat at the edge of my bed and put on my shoes, trying to think if there was *any* way I could get out of this. If I pretended to get sick now, it would be too obvious. I *had* to go.

It was beyond unfair that I was forced to go when I hadn't even wanted to be nominated. I sighed, for the millionth time this week, and stood, grabbing my clutch.

"Ready?" Paige asked, her cheeks flushed even through the blush.

"Ready," I said.

Not.

24

SMILE!

PAIGE AND I WALKED DOWN THE HALLWAY, Paige's heels click-clacking on the floor. We passed Jas's empty room. At least she wasn't here to attend the dance.

Paige and I waved at Livvie, the Winchester dorm monitor, as we passed her office.

"Oh, wait a sec!" Livvie called after us.

We stopped and Livvie appeared in her doorway, camera in hand.

"I can't let you girls leave without a picture," she said. "It's the first time you've attended Homecoming and I want you to have something to look at later to help you remember this very special night."

Last year, I'd been too overwhelmed to participate, and Paige had been too busy.

I almost rolled my eyes when she said "special," but I stopped myself.

Livvie put the camera in front of her and zoomed the lens at us. "Get together, girls," she said. "And smile."

Obediently, I placed my arm around Paige's waist and she slung hers over my shoulder. We smiled at Livvie.

"One . . . two . . . three!" Livvie pushed a button and her camera flash nearly blinded me.

"I'll e-mail a copy to your parents," she said. "I'm sure they'll be excited to see a pic of you both in your dresses."

Paige nodded enthusiastically. "My parents will love it."

"Mine too," I said. And they would. They had no idea about any of the Eric/Callie/Jacob mess and whenever we'd talked or texted, I'd told Mom and Dad that I was excited about fall break and had ignored as much talk about Homecoming as possible. I didn't want them to know what was going on—it would lead to endless questions from Mom and Dad and they would only worry.

"And I'll send a copy to the administration office. They like to use photos like these for the view books of students considering enrolling at Canterwood," Livvie said. She waved us off and we left Winchester.

Instead of chatting, Paige was quiet. I knew that meant

she was nervous. I bumped her arm with my elbow.

"Things are going to be fine with Ryan," I said. "Don't worry or overanalyze. You're going to be great. Plus, you're *royalty* at this event, Paige. You were nominated for Homecoming princess!"

That made Paige smile. "Omigod, what if either of us win? That would be amazing!"

We approached the ballroom and I looked at her sideways. "Admit it. You just want that tiara."

Paige laughed. "Okay, okay. I kind of do. It's just so sparkly!"

"Well, when you win it, you have to share. Otherwise, I'll have to steal it from you.'"

"I won't win, but if I do, I'll definitely share. And the same rule applies to you."

We reached the ballroom and a massive Canterwood Crest banner hung over the doorway. The green banner had the school's name and crest stitched into it. The black railing was trimmed with green and gold ribbon and the usually bright white light bulbs that were in lanterns on either side of the door had been changed to a softer yellow. The glow made the entrance look almost golden.

Paige pulled open one of the glass doors and we stepped into the lobby. We took the hallway that led to

the ballroom and Paige and I halted in the doorway. The massive room with its arched windows, hardwood floors and creamy off-white walls looked nothing like the ballroom I'd seen before. Green and gold were *everywhere*.

A green carpet ran from the doorway to the food and drink tables. Gold glitter was sprinkled over the white table clothes. On one table, there were silver buckets with sparkling grape juice and other fun drinks.

The floor had been buffed to a soft sheen and the room had Canterwood Crest posters and crests on the walls. I pulled Paige over to a narrow wall between two windows and couldn't stop staring.

"Omigosh," I said. "Did you do this?"

The wall had been turned into a collage. It had black and white candid photos of what looked like everyone in seventh and eighth grade. I scanned the pictures—spotting the ones of my friends. A picture of Paige and Geena peering into their mixing bowls in cooking class and wearing aprons made me smile. Nicole, with an arm slung over Wish's shoulder, grinned at the camera. There were shots of Troy, Andy, and Ben laughing in the caf at their table. A photo of the Trio, with their heads together in the Orchard common room, captured them perfectly.

Then I saw a picture of Callie and Jacob. She held his

hand and looked into his eyes, her complete attention on him. Jacob, though, was looking just over her shoulder. They were sitting in the courtyard near the fountain. His gaze was so intense—I wondered what he was looking at.

There was a great photo of Eric in the outdoor arena. He was riding Luna, the school horse he used for lessons, and they were in midair over a jump. His form was perfect and it made my throat close a little to think about how we used to coach each other and practice together.

"There you are," Paige said. She pointed to a pic in the middle. I was sitting by myself on a bench by the courtyard, reading something in my English notebook. In the far side of the picture, three girls were clustered together, laughing and smiling. I peered closer at them.

Rachel and her friends.

I looked away from Rachel and my eyes stopped on another picture. Callie and I sitting on a bench in the courtyard with an enormous stack of books between us. I flashed back, remembering that moment when we'd been cramming last minute for midterms. Back when we'd been friends.

I turned away from the wall. "I'm starving. Let's eat."

Paige and I walked down the green carpet and started

toward the drink table. I kept my eyes on the food table—not wanting to see Eric, Jacob, or Callie if they were already here.

"Did you pick out all of this food?" I asked Paige. "It's fantastic."

Paige shrugged, smiling. "I chose most of it. The catering staff cooked everything—Geena and I just told them what we wanted."

Tables were lined from end to end with crystal plates filled with food. There was a table of fun food—pigs in a blanket, mini corn dogs, nachos and cheese, and hamburger sliders. Another table had more sophisticated food—quiches, roast beef and pepper kabobs, shrimp, and a few other different varieties of meats, cheeses, and breads.

I grabbed a green plastic plate—customized with CCA in gold in the center—and got in line. "You know I'm going to have at least one of everything."

"Me too. Let's get some food and grab drinks." Paige scanned the room as she took a plate. "I don't see Ryan yet."

"He'll be here," I reassured her. "He wants to see you and he's nominated for prince, so don't worry."

Paige and I filled our plates and poured glasses of

sparkling white grape juice. Paige glanced around the room again and she spun back around to look at me, almost sloshing juice over the side of her glass.

"He's here!" she said. "Ryan's here!"

"Go say hi," I said. "I'm going to be eating anyway. I'll go find Nicole or someone to hang with for a while."

Paige stared at me. "You sure? You can totally come over with us."

"I'm sure. Go." I gently shoved Paige away from me.

She tossed one last look over her shoulder and I waved her away. I wanted her to spend Homecoming with Ryan. I also didn't want to keep up my fake *Oh, Homecoming rocks!* act much longer. If I wasn't around Paige, then I could relax a little.

One of the guys in my math class was the DJ. He cranked the volume up a notch louder. A pop-rock mix streamed from the speakers and people started dancing in the center of the floor in front of the stage. Ugh. Soon, I'd be on that stage as the winners of the junior royal court were announced.

Ignore it, I told myself. I walked to the edge of the room and found an empty seat away from the food and drink tables. I hadn't seen Callie, Eric, or Jacob yet, so at least I didn't have to keep an eye on them.

I went for the dessert first and took a bite of my vanilla cupcake with gold frosting.

"Silver."

I looked up, midbite. Heather stood in front of me.

"I'm going to ditch you right now if you don't wipe that ridiculous frosting off your face," Heather said. She rolled her blue eyes.

I swiped at my mouth with my napkin. "When did you get here?"

"Just now. Julia and Alison were freaking out because they didn't want to miss one second of it and Alison had a last-minute shoe emergency."

"What happened?"

Heather sat on the chair beside me. "Her heel broke. She was devastated. As if they were the only pair of shoes she had to wear."

"Paige had a shoe moment too," I said. "But I get it. They want to look amazing—they think Homecoming is a big deal."

"True." Heather nodded down at her own dark blue halter dress. "I dressed up, but I didn't go crazy."

"Me either. And it was kind of nice for once not to have that crazy pressure of dressing up and worrying about my date and all that stuff."

"This is just an annoyance," Heather said, sighing. "We're here against our will *and* we have to watch girls throw themselves at guys. Like I'd ever do that."

I looked sideways at her. We'd never talked about boys—only when she'd pretended to go after Jacob.

"Was there someone you wanted to go with?" I asked. I sat back in my chair a little, expecting her to snap at me and tell me it was none of my business.

Heather stared at her hands in her lap, then looked over at me. "I wouldn't have minded if Troy had asked me to go with him."

I tried not to let my mouth flop open. Heather had a crush *and* she was insecure about it. For once, she didn't have all the answers. She wanted something but didn't know how to go after it.

Total. Shocker.

"Troy's great," I said, keeping my voice calm. "Does he know you like him?"

Heather shrugged. "I'm not sure. We talk at the stable a lot, but it's always casual conversation about riding. I think he might like me, but I don't know."

"Maybe you could find out tonight. Get something out of being here. More than whatever your mom got out of it."

I looked over and saw Troy standing with Andy and a couple of the riders from the seventh-grade intermediate team.

"He's over there," I said, tipping my chin in his direction.

Heather looked over at Troy. She ran her fingers through her hair and stood. "Back in a sec."

"Good luck," I said. I smiled to myself and watched her maneuver through the crowd toward Troy. I finished my food and stood to throw away my plate. I found a trash can near the back of the room and tossed in my plate. When I turned, Jacob stood in front of me—hands in his pockets. He wore black pants, a blazer, and a gray T-shirt. He looked amazing.

I clutched my cup and stared at him.

"You look beautiful," he said. His voice was soft and his green eyes met mine.

"Thanks," I said. I was barely able to get out the word. Even though he was single and I wasn't with Eric, it felt wrong to talk to him. But I *so* wanted to. And I hated how confused I felt. If I cared about Callie's feelings like I claimed, I would stay away from Jacob and not even think about us ever being together. But I couldn't stop what I felt—no matter how hard I tried.

"You're going to win," Jacob said. "There's no way anyone else could be Homecoming princess."

I shook my head. "But I don't want to be a princess! I just want to get out of here."

"Because of Callie, Eric, and me."

I paused, then nodded. "We all have to be onstage together. Every time I see Callie she looks like she wants to kill me. Eric just ignores me—not that he doesn't have every right to. And you—" I caught myself.

"What?"

Jacob stepped closer and I could almost feel his breath on my face. I took a step back.

"Nothing," I said. "We can't be talking like this. People already think I'm a horrible person who stole my best friend's boyfriend. It's only going to make it worse if they see us talking now."

"Sasha, you have to know why I broke up with Callie."

I glanced down at the floor, then back at him. "Why?"

"I couldn't do it, Sash. I couldn't stay with her when I wasn't feeling it. The longer I was with her, the harder it would have been when we finally broke up."

I squeezed my eyes shut. "I get that—I do. I know you were saving her from more pain later, but it's still hard to see her now."

"I feel awful that I hurt her. She's a great girl," Jacob said. "I told her that I was too overwhelmed with school, sports, and everything else to be a good boyfriend. She was hurt, but I know she believed it. She *never* thought it was because of what happened at your party."

"Are you sure?" I rubbed the back of my neck. "Jacob, I don't want her to ever doubt that what she had with you was real. You were her *first* boyfriend. She has to keep hating me."

"That's not fair to you," Jacob said. "She was your best friend and you're taking the blame for what *I* did. You could tell her the truth and be friends again."

I shook my head. "I can't."

And I knew the other reason I wasn't saying—I didn't want Jacob to be the bad guy. I cared about him too much to expose what he'd done.

Jacob's eyes searched my face. "If you're not going to try to work things out with Callie, then she can be mad at both of us . . . together."

"Jacob." I wrapped my arms across my chest.

"Sasha." He said my name in the same tone I'd said his. "I know we can't right now, but you want to eventually." He paused. "Right?"

"W-we can't," I said, stumbling over my words. I had

to pull it together or he'd know I was lying. "It would be obvious to Callie that you broke up with her for me and it would *kill* her. We've already done enough to her."

Jacob put a warm hand on my forearm. "Callie will move on. She'll find another boyfriend. You know she'll be okay. I want *you* to be happy too. And I think I could make you happy. I want to try."

I froze.

I wanted to tell him yes. Wanted to say that I wanted to try after we waited a while.

"It's not just about Callie," I said. "I want—I need— to be single. I just made the YENT and I've got to focus."

I blinked, trying not to cry, and knew I had to go before I changed my mind.

Jacob looked down at his shoes and I glanced over his shoulder.

My eyes connected with someone else's.

25

WHOSE MOVE?

ERIC.

He stared at me, his beautiful brown eyes searching my face. My stomach swirled and, for a second, I was unaware that I was standing just feet away from Jacob.

"What're you staring at?" Jacob asked.

He turned and saw Eric.

Eric's face changed in an instant. It was as if he expected to see me here with Jacob. To see us this close together, even though we weren't doing anything.

I paused—unsure what to do.

Then Rachel appeared by Eric's side. The pretty seventh grader had swept her light brown hair into a twist and her sideswept bangs made her look sophisticated. Rosy blush complemented her coloring and the light freckles that were sprinkled across her nose.

She looked at me and gave me an odd half wave. I didn't even know how to respond. Before I could, Eric slipped his hand into Rachel's and led her away from Jacob and me. She leaned into him as they walked and I felt a little stab of jealousy. I could never be with Eric— not after what I'd done to him. But seeing him with *Rachel* was harder than I'd thought. She and her group of friends seemed to be more of a presence on campus lately and she was spending more time with the eighth graders than the seventh graders.

I looked back at Jacob, envisioning him walking away hand in hand with another girl. It was more than I could even think about.

"I've got to go," I mumbled. "See you onstage."

I walked away from Jacob, losing myself in the crowd. Everyone was dancing to the music and it was easy to hide myself among them. I stayed away from the food and drink tables, where everyone seemed to gather at some point, and mixed in with a group of people I didn't know.

My eyes stopped on Eric and Rachel. They were dancing together and Eric was smiling at her—the smile that

he'd once given me. She gazed adoringly at him. Her friends, back at the drinks table, giggled and whispered.

The music faded, then stopped. The lights on the stage brightened and everyone turned to watch Headmistress Drake walk across the stage and step up to the microphone.

"Hello, students," she said. She smiled at us.

"It's now time to announce the winners of the eighth-grade junior royal court. Will the eighth-grade nominees please come onstage?"

I stood still—waiting to see who would make the first move.

26

CROWNED

I SAW CALLIE MOVE THROUGH THE CROWD. It was the first time I'd seen her all night. She looked stunning in a deep purple V-neck cap-sleeve dress with black kitten heels. Callie walked to the side of the stage, climbed the stairs, and stood behind Headmistress Drake. Nicole was onstage next, then the guys started to line up a few feet away from the girls. Jacob and Eric stood at opposite ends of their line, just like Callie and I did. Paige hurried to stand next to me and Heather took her time getting onstage and stood on my other side.

The spotlight was blinding. I couldn't see anyone in the crowd, but I was glad—I wanted to pretend that no one else was in the room. The people onstage were enough to deal with.

Headmistress Drake smiled at us, then turned back to the crowd. "Please give a round of applause to your eighth-grade junior royal court nominees."

Everyone clapped for what felt like *forever*.

"Thank you," Headmistress Drake said. "The students standing before you are those who were nominated by you. One boy and one girl will be crowned prince and princess of the eighth-grade junior royal court. This is an enormous honor that only a select few students at Canterwood Crest Academy ever experience during their time here."

Omigod, how much longer was she going to talk?!

"The level of commitment to our school that I've observed this week made me even more proud of our student body. Each of you threw yourself into all aspects of Homecoming and your dedication to our institution is inspiring."

Headmistress Drake paused and smiled at the crowd.

"I've talked enough," she said. "I realize you're all anxious to hear your winners. Just a reminder—the winners and runners-up will dance together."

At least I didn't have to worry about that. I had to make it through the announcements. Then the plan was to sneak out.

"And your runners-up for eighth-grade junior royal court are . . ."

I looked over at Heather, who blinked, looking bored. I sneaked a glance at Paige. Her hands were clasped together and her eyes were wide and gleaming in the stage light.

"Eric Rodriguez and Sasha Silver!" Headmistress Drake said.

Omigodomigodomigod. I started to sway and, for a second, I thought Fainting Sasha might make an appearance.

"Hold it together, Silver," Heather hissed in my ear. "Just stand there."

I couldn't even make myself look past Heather to see what the guys' reactions were. I didn't want to see Eric's face. He had to be just as unhappy about the idea of being forced to dance with me.

Cheers of "Go, Eric!" and "Yeah!" broke out from the crowd. Paige reached over and squeezed my arm.

"Congratulations!" she said, beaming at me. I just stared at her. Did she *not* realize what I was feeling?

I didn't answer Paige—I looked back at the crowd and tried to breathe.

"And your winners for the eighth-grade junior royal court are . . ." Headmistress Drake said. "Jacob Schwartz and Heather Fox!"

Heather's head snapped around in my direction and her face had a look I'm sure was similar to mine when I'd heard my name.

"Hold it together," I said, repeating her words. "You're the Homecoming princess."

The crowd cheered and the clapping seemed to reverberate from the walls.

"My mother is going to freak," Heather whispered, with an amused expression. "Omigod. This is *beyond* wrong."

I smiled, shaking my head, then looked over at Paige.

"You should have won," I whispered.

Paige managed a smile, but I could see the disappointment on her face. "It's okay. I wanted to win, but at least I still get to dance with Ryan."

"Exactly," I said.

Headmistress Drake turned to face us. "Please congratulate your winners. When you're finished, Eric, Sasha, Heather, and Jacob need to head down to the center of the floor."

Before I could move, Nicole came over and hugged me. "Congratulations," she said. "I'm so happy for you!"

"Thanks," I whispered.

Nicole started to reach out to hug Heather, but when she got a glimpse of Heather's face, she yanked her arms back.

"Um, congratulations, Heather," Nicole said, flashing a smile. Heather glared at her and stalked off to the other side of the stage. Nicole walked feet behind her, keeping a careful distance.

I looked over and Headmistress Drake was still watching us—making sure the winners were properly congratulated. If she wasn't watching, I'd *so* be off this stage.

Paige walked over to the other nominees. I was hyperaware that Callie and I were the only two girls standing at our end of the stage.

Callie straightened her shoulders and walked over, stopping directly in front of me. Her dark eyes bore into mine and she almost didn't even look like my ex–best friend.

"Congratulations, Sasha," Callie said, her voice cold.

"Thanks," I said. I opened my mouth, wanting to say something—but not knowing what to say. Before I could decide, Callie walked away.

Headmistress Drake would call me out for being a poor sport if I didn't walk over to the other side.

Just get it over with, I told myself.

I walked over and Troy reached me first. "Congratulations, Sash," he said.

"Thanks," I said.

Andy and Ben cast a quick glance at Eric before coming over to me.

"Congrats, almost-princess," Andy said, smiling at me.

Ben nodded. "Yeah, I'm glad you placed. That's cool."

I listened to them, but it was almost as if I couldn't hear their words. I couldn't stop watching Eric and Jacob. They had no reason to talk, but I couldn't help worrying that Jacob would try to do what he thought was right and tell Eric and Callie the truth about my party. *But he promised he wouldn't,* I reminded myself. And I trusted Jacob.

Eric and Jacob stood as far away from each other as possible. Callie was talking to Eric and Nicole and Jacob were engaged in conversation.

I looked around for Heather and saw her talking to Troy. She smiled at him and he grinned back at her. Maybe the bright spot of the night was the possibility that this could be the start of something between them.

Callie walked away from Eric and left the stage. Eric was alone now—it was the perfect time to talk. Then, after I congratulated Jacob, I could leave the stage.

I took a looong breath and walked over to Eric. He looked comfortable dressed up in a black blazer, black pants, and a red button-down shirt. But he looked like he would have rather been wearing a polo shirt and breeches.

I walked up to his side and when his scent hit me—the smell of clean laundry mixed with mint—it was overwhelming. He turned to look at me and I almost stepped back when our eyes met.

"Congratulations," I said. My voice was barely audible over the crowd on the floor that had burst into chatter.

"You too," he said. Unlike Callie, there wasn't a hint of malice or anger in his voice. That was Eric. Calm. Acting as if this was completely fine that we were about to dance together. The way he handled these situations made me hope we could be friends one day.

"I guess I'll see you on the floor," I said.

He nodded and his eyes left my face when Jacob walked over.

"See you there," Eric said to me. He looked at Jacob. "Congrats."

Jacob nodded. "You too."

Eric disappeared offstage and I was left standing with Jacob. I wanted to hurry off the stage and stand next to him at the same time.

He looked at me, shaking his head. "Can you believe this?" he asked. "I have to dance with Heather and you get . . ." He could barely get out the name. ". . . Eric."

"I know. It's so not fair. If we're 'princes' and 'princesses,' why can't we do whatever we want?"

"If I got to do what I wanted," Jacob said, leaning closer. "I'd dance with you all night."

I looked at him—saying nothing but wanting to spill everything. The ache I had in my chest whenever I saw Eric intensified times a million when I looked at Jacob. I wanted everything to be simple—I wanted Eric to be happy with whomever he chose, I wanted Callie back as my best friend and, maybe most of all, I wanted a chance with Jacob. I wanted him to be my boyfriend. My video-game-playing, Nintendo-obsessed, afraid-of-horses boyfriend. I wanted to tell him all of that. But I couldn't.

"I have to go," I said.

"I know." Jacob's eyes were on mine and we'd somehow moved so close to each other that our faces were inches apart. Jacob smelled like chocolate frosting and cupcakes. Even that tiny detail made me miss him. And I couldn't handle thinking about it.

Before I lost it, I walked across the stage and down the stairs.

Eric was waiting in the center of the floor. Without a word, he reached out and took my hand in his warm one.

Feet away, Jacob and Heather held each other's hands. Heather looked over at me and I shot her a *Can you believe this?* look over Eric's shoulder.

The lights dimmed and a semislow song started. Eric was a wonderful dancer. He didn't glare at me or try to make me any more uncomfortable than I already was. And that was something I liked and missed about him. We'd been able to talk to each other about anything. He'd made me hot chocolate the night Jacob and I had gotten into a screaming match at the Sweetheart Soirée. He'd coached me through the YENT tryouts—being there for me through all of my insecurities.

And I'd thought it was enough. I'd been beyond happy. When Eric had misinterpreted what he'd seen between Jacob and me, I thought I'd be devastated for months about losing Eric. And I was—I missed his presence in my life. His friendship. I couldn't stop thinking about Jacob, but I had to stay single.

I kept my gaze over Eric's shoulder and he did the same, looking over mine. Heather and Jacob were keeping a polite distance between them and they weren't looking at each other either.

The minutes seemed to drag on forever and finally, the song ended. The crowd clapped and Eric released my hands. I didn't know what to do or what to say. Did I just walk away?

"Excuse me," Heather said. She stepped between Eric and me. "I'm cutting in."

Heather grabbed my arm and led me away. "You need to dance with the guy you really like," she said. "Jacob."

27
SAVED

"THANKS FOR SAVING ME," I SAID TO Heather. "But I can't dance with Jacob."

"Why?" she asked. "You're both single."

I shook my head. "It doesn't matter. I still have a tiny bit of hope that Callie and I will somehow be able to be friends again one day and if I date her ex-boyfriend after she thinks I broke them up, there's no way we'll ever be friends again."

"But what about you?" Heather nodded slowly. "And Jacob?"

I shrugged.

"Don't, Silver. You both want to be together. It's not even an excuse to say you won't be with him because of Callie. If you really wanted Callie back, you'd tell her the truth—that Jacob went after you."

"But—"

"But you won't," Heather interrupted. "Because you don't want to make him look bad. I know. You've said. But if you did, then you'd get Callie back and she'd just hate Jacob, not you."

"I know you're trying to help, but I don't want to keep talking about this. It's just not going to happen between Jacob and me. It can't."

Heather stared at me, shaking her head.

"Excuse me," Paige said, stepping beside us. "I need to talk to Sasha."

Heather shrugged. "Talk."

"Alone," Paige said.

"Fine. Talk *alone*," Heather said, mocking Paige's tone. She looked at me one more time before walking away.

"Can we talk for a sec?" Paige asked. "Somewhere more quiet?"

"Sure."

But I wasn't sure at all. I followed Paige to the back of the room and my stomach twisted before she spoke a word. Paige was obviously upset and I had no idea what this was about.

We found an empty corner and Paige turned to me.

"Sasha, I noticed something tonight," Paige said.

"What?" I asked.

Paige took a long breath. "You and Jacob. You've been looking at each other all night. Glances here and there. Long stares. He's been watching you and you can't take your eyes off him."

"That's so not true," I said. "Yeah, we talked for a minute. But we had to—Headmistress Drake made us congratulate the winners. You heard her."

Paige rubbed her forehead with her hand. "I feel like I've been living with someone else since your party. You just told me the truth about what happened with him—don't start lying now. There's something going on and you keep shutting me out. I want to know why. Right now."

28

MAKE THE CALL

I WASN'T GOING TO HAVE THIS CONVERSATION here. No way was I going to be that girl who had drama at another school event.

"If you want to talk, let's go to the bathroom," I said. "We don't need to talk about this out here."

"Fine."

Paige and I walked out of the ballroom and entered the bathroom just down the hallway. We pushed open the heavy wooden door and I listened for a second to hear if anyone else was inside, but we were alone. I leaned up against the sand-colored marble sink and Paige put her purse on the small couch near the full-length mirror.

"I *cannot* keep doing this," I said. "I told you the truth—Jacob made a move on me at my party. I didn't try to kiss him. But it doesn't mean I'm going to get back together with him. We might be looking at each other, or whatever you think is going on, but that's it. We're never going to be boyfriend and girlfriend."

"You're protecting him because you like him," Paige said. "Otherwise, you'd tell Callie the truth. I get it."

"Do you?" I asked. "Because you dragged me away from Heather to 'talk' and you don't seem to get it at all. This whole Homecoming thing has been in my face so much and you didn't seem to understand. You left me standing by the bonfire to go help your precious committee."

Paige shook her head. "I apologized for that. I told you I was wrong. But you know what? I don't think this has anything to do with Homecoming."

We eyed each other and I folded my arms. "Enlighten me, please."

"You're jealous that I'm with Ryan and you don't have a boyfriend."

I stared at her—stunned. "Are you *kidding* me, Paige? Seriously?"

Paige just shrugged. She was being crazy!

"I'm *thrilled* that you're with Ryan!" I half shouted. "I can't believed you'd ever think anything else. Who was the one who pushed you to talk to him? Who helped you send the e-mail for the group date? Who helped you get ready for your first date?" I stepped away from her, shaking my head. "Enjoy your wonderful, amazing Homecoming dance. It's been your number one priority all week, so don't stop now. I'm out of here."

I turned away and started for the door.

"Sasha, wait." Paige's voice was high. "I didn't mean—"

"And you know what," I interrupted. "I think we need some time apart."

"What are you talking about?" Paige's face paled.

"I'm going to stay here for break," I said. "You go home and I'll stay in our room. We need space and we can talk after break."

"Sasha." Paige's voice was wavery. "I want you to come home with me. You can't stay on campus by yourself. I shouldn't have—"

I shook my head and cut her off. "I'm staying here. I'm going to go back to our room and call my parents."

I walked out of the bathroom and headed down the hallway. I'd been at the dance long enough and I didn't care if I got in trouble for leaving.

"You okay?"

I turned and Heather walked toward me.

"Not really," I said. "Paige and I had a huge fight. She

accused me of something ridiculous and I can't be around her right now." I sighed and rubbed my forehead. "I was supposed to stay with Paige for break, but I'm going to stay here."

"Well, that only sounds like the lamest fall break ever. At least I'm going home with a ridic tiara."

"What else am I supposed to do?" I snapped. "I'm not going to stay with Paige. Sorry if that sounds 'lame' to you."

"It *is* lame. You're just planning to hide in your room all week and do what?"

"I don't know! Stuff—whatever." I rolled my eyes. "I'm out of here. I've got to go call my parents and tell them where I'm staying."

I stepped around Heather and started down the hallway.

"Sasha," Heather called.

"What?" I turned and looked at her.

"When you call them, tell them you're staying with me."

I'd *definitely* heard her wrong.

"What?" I repeated.

"You're staying with me," Heather said. "Make the call."

ABOUT THE AUTHOR

Twenty-three-year-old Jessica Burkhart is a writer from New York City. Like Sasha, she's crazy about horses, lip gloss, and all things pink and sparkly. Jess was an equestrian and had a horse like Charm before she started writing. To watch Jess's vlogs and read her blog, visit www.jessicaburkhart.com.

Real life. Real you.

Total Knockout

Don't miss
any of these
terrific
Aladdin Mix
books.

Home Sweet Drama

This Is Me From Now On

Devon Delaney Should
Totally Know Better

Front Page Face-Off

Four Truths and a Lie

Sometimes a girl just needs a good book.
Lauren Barnholdt understands.

MEET BRITTANY, CASSIE, AND ISABEL.
THREE GIRLS WITH BIG DREAMS
AND BIG AMBITIONS.

Sometimes the drama during the commercials is better than what happens during the show. And sometimes the drama making the commercial is even better. . . .

DOUBLE TROUBLE JUST TOOK ON a WHOLE new meaning....